# Novels by Kelly Cheek

All We Hold Dear
Trial by Fire
The Lost Colony
JackSimile and the Phantom Fury
Spirit Breather

## The SpiritSense Trilogy

In Restless Dreams
First Light
When We Were Gone Astray

## The Facebook Trilogy

Profile
Private Messages
Poked

# WHEN WE WERE
# GONE ASTRAY

Kelly Cheek

Cover and book design by Kelly Cheek

ISBN: 978-1-7335022-6-9

Printed in the United States of America

God shall not pity them but laugh at their calamity. The righteous company in heaven shall rejoice in the execution of God's judgment, and shall sing while the smoke riseth up for ever.

– Thomas Boston


But the fearful, and unbelieving, and the abominable, and murderers, and whoremongers, and sorcerers, and idolaters, and all liars, shall have their part in the lake which burneth with fire and brimstone: which is the second death.

– Revelation 21:8

# 1

Fin MacKinley clicked "Send" in his e-mail program and watched with a sense of satisfaction as his manuscript was whisked away to his editor. His satisfaction was short-lived, though. He wished he had someone to share the moment with.

He yawned. It had been a long night. Knowing he was almost finished with the novel, he had lain awake for a good portion of the night with different versions of the ending going through his head. He had thought about getting up and finishing it then, but he was a man who liked his routines. Night was for sleeping. So, he waited until the morning, and he was glad he did. The extra time spent pondering the ending yielded one that he especially liked.

"Hey Suzy," he typed into his phone, "I finished it. It's on its way to my editor."

He looked out the window near his desk in his library, through the softly falling snow, at the one house he could see from here. He wondered what a *normal* person would do upon this momentous milestone, the completion of his latest novel. He had a pretty good idea, and the thought of it made him shudder. Perhaps calling a few friends and meeting at a noisy, crowded bar for drinks to celebrate the occasion.

He wondered if the Andersons, the family in the house he could see, would be considered normal. He wasn't even sure what constituted normalcy.

He turned and looked at the lights in the corner. He had put up his Christmas tree in his library, since it was the room he spent the most time in. The tree was a small one, hardly worth the trouble, but he didn't see the point in elaborate decorations. He was going to be spending Christmas alone.

Fin was a frustrated New York Times bestselling author with one successful film adaptation so far, and a promising one still in the works. He was frustrated partly because, despite his success, he was anonymous. He wrote under the pseudonym Michael Jones. Fin MacKinley was, as far as the world was concerned, a nobody.

He was also an introvert, so he was conflicted. He longed for the fame and celebrity, and the recognition for his accomplishments.

At the same time, he dreaded it.

He watched his phone for a few moments, but there was no reply. He sighed and looked back out the window. The snow was still falling. It looked like it was about four inches deep by now.

He had met Suzy Quinn a little over two years ago, a few weeks after their first contact through a genealogy site, of all things. Since then, their relationship had progressed far beyond genealogical links. Not that they were related. But their respective distant ancestors had known each other and had dealings of a somewhat questionable nature.

During their online contact, though, as well as during a trip to Scotland, and Suzy's visit to Colorado in April, they had fallen in love. Still, the death of Suzy's husband and daughter three years ago had proven an obstacle to furthering their relationship. Fin was frustrated. Suzy was perplexed.

Fin sighed and slipped his phone back into the holster on his belt. It didn't help that this Christmas season was going to be a lonely one. Not that he knew any other kind.

He had tried to convince Suzy to come to Colorado, or to let him visit her at her place. But she said that she was going to be busy and couldn't pull herself away.

He yawned again, and he shook his head. He thought it was too early for a nap, but maybe after a walk out in the snow.

Pushing himself up from his chair, he went downstairs to his walkout basement. He opened the closet near his back door and got out a parka. A slight movement on the sleeve caught his eye, and in a panic, he dropped the coat. The spider fell off the sleeve and onto the tile floor. Living where he lived, finding bugs in his house was a common occurrence. While Fin was nothing like Jeff Daniels' character in *Arachnophobia*, spiders just gave him a creepy feeling.

He had been accustomed to killing spiders when he found them, but Suzy had convinced him to put them outside instead of killing them. Knowing what the weather was like now, though, he knew that it would be a death sentence anyway. *At least this is quicker*, he thought as he stepped on the spider. With a tissue from the nearby half bath, he wiped up the remains from the tile, then put on his parka. Time to get outside for a bit.

*All work and no play makes Jack a dull boy*, he thought. Then, he shook his head.

*Damn, I can't even think up original lines. Now I'm stealing from Stephen King.*

He stepped outside and gasped at the brisk temperature. It was cold, but the clouds overhead were bright. The snow would probably stop soon.

The snow, the cold temperature, and the line from *The Shining*, made him shiver, recalling how that story turned out for Jack Torrance. He remembered how, last spring, he had suggested to Suzy that they go to the Stanley Hotel up in Estes Park. The Stanley Hotel was Stephen King's inspiration for The Overlook Hotel in *The Shining*, and he thought it would be cool if she could apply her unique talent to the ghosts haunting The Stanley. Her reason for declining had been sound, but the memory of the occasion added a fresh pang to his loneliness.

Suzy lived in Marblehead, a quaint old village on the shore of Massachusetts, just a few miles north of Boston. Her family's estate was packed to the gills with memories of her dead husband and daughter.

As if the two thousand miles separating them weren't bad enough.

Fin lived on the edge of a sparse neighborhood southwest of the urban and suburban sprawl of Denver, Colorado, in the last little community before the foothills and forest took over. The developer who built the houses had run out of money before completing his envisioned contribution to the sprawl. So, besides the sporadic spacing of homes, the development failed to attract the compulsory trappings of civilization – strip malls, grocery stores, gas stations, restaurants, bars.

Fin was fine with that. It simply assured that his home remained somewhat secluded. Being an introvert, that was important to him.

Still, he got lonely from time to time, and more so lately. But his loneliness couldn't be assuaged by just spending time with other people in general. His was a very specific loneliness.

He missed Suzy.

§

As expected, the snow stopped a few minutes after Fin started his walk. With each step, he enjoyed the satisfying squinch, Fin's word for the squeaky crunch of the snow under his feet.

Also as expected, the clouds gradually parted and the sun came out. When it did, he quickly turned around and started heading back. He knew the likely result of staying out in these conditions. He mentally kicked himself for not bringing sunglasses.

As the sunlight shone on the freshly fallen snow, the brightness became intense, and he felt the stab of a knife behind his right eye from the fierce white light. Fin knew that he needed to retreat to the relative darkness of his house, before a full-fledged migraine set in. He kept to the trees as long as he could, making use of what shade they afforded, protecting his eyes as much as possible.

Suddenly, he stopped, standing completely still, closing his eyes and concentrating. With no more squinching, the silence was profound. Straining his ears, he heard it again, a tiny, squeaky little sound, from back in the forest.

Fin turned and went in that direction, making fresh tracks as he went off the trail, and into the welcome shade of the denser trees. Hearing the sound again, he adjusted his bearing. Then he saw it, a fuzzy little teddy bear struggling under a tree.

It saw him as he approached, and seemed to get excited, bouncing up and down. It was a little dog, a Pomeranian, he thought, its fur caught in the bramble tangled around the base of a pine.

"Hey, little guy," he said in a voice that people reserve for when they're talking to dogs and cats and children. He squatted down beside the dog. "Looks like you've gotten yourself in a little bit of a pickle."

He knelt down beside the dog and began gently picking its fur from the thorns, getting a few scrapes and pokes of his own in the process. When at last the little dog was free, it bounded around Fin, celebrating his savior, kicking up plumes of snow around it.

"Okay," Fin laughed, "settle down." He gently picked up the dog. There were some spots of blood on its fur. Fin figured they were probably just scrapes from the thorns, but he wanted to be able to examine the dog a little more thoroughly, to make sure the blood wasn't from more serious injuries. He felt in the thick fur around the dog's neck, but there was no collar, no identification.

He stood up and held the dog in one arm, tucking it against his body like a football, though the sports simile didn't occur to him. As he held the dog and started walking back toward his house, the dog relaxed and stayed completely still in his arm.

As he emerged from the shade of the forest, he shaded his eyes with his other hand, making it back to his house before the pain became too intense. Once he got inside and closed the door, he sighed with relief as the headache eased a bit. Still, it was there, throbbing on the right side of his head.

He put the dog down and shed his coat, heading to the bathroom near the back door where he kept a bottle of the nose spray. Snorting a shot up each nostril, the relief was almost instantaneous. He sighed as he put the bottle back in the medicine cabinet. He turned toward the dog, which was watching him curiously from the doorway.

"So," Fin said, as the dog tilted its head to the side, "where did you come from?"

He pulled his phone from its holster and scrolled down a couple of names in his short list of contacts. He had the number of the Andersons, his closest neighbors, in his phone, but he hadn't had any interaction with them in months, other than waving at them in passing. He had trusted them enough that they had exchanged house keys a few years ago, in case of emergency, but so far, there had been no need for either of them to use them.

"Marian," Fin said as soon as she answered, "it's Fin, next door."

They exchanged greetings, and Fin, uncomfortable with most small talk, got right to the point.

"You don't happen to be missing a little dog, do you?"

"A little dog?"

"Yeah, I found a dog in the forest, tangled up in a thorn bush. It looks like a Pomeranian, cute as can be, but it doesn't have a collar."

"No, it's not ours," Marian replied. "We have two indoor cats, but no dogs."

"Do you know of anybody else who might be missing a dog?" Fin asked.

"Let's see," she pondered aloud, "the Millers have a couple of bigger dogs, but I'm pretty sure they don't have a little one. And besides, they're in Arizona for the winter. The Turners, in the house next to me, have a dog, but I know he's not lost, because I can hear him yapping to get in. So no, I can't think of anybody around here that it would belong to."

"Okay," Fin sighed. "Thanks."

"Why don't you try taking it to a vet?"

"A vet?"

"Sure. The vet could scan it to see if it has a chip. If it does, you could call the owner and reunite them."

"That's a good idea. Thanks, Marian!"

§

"I'm afraid there's no chip," Dr. Horst said.

Fin had looked up Google Maps to find the nearest vet. The receptionist said that, due to the weather, they had a couple of cancellations, so he could bring the dog in right away. Dr. Mike Horst looked like he was about seventeen years old, but he had a wedding ring on his finger, and he was a licensed vet, so Fin figured he was probably older than he looked.

"Damn!" Fin said under his breath. He sighed and looked at the vet. "What do you think I should do?"

"You want a dog?" Fin raised his eyebrows, and Dr. Horst smiled. "You could make up some flyers and put them up around your neighborhood."

"Actually, I live in a pretty small and remote neighborhood," Fin replied, looking down at the dog. The dog sat on the metal-topped examining table, watching Fin, her reddish-gold fur gleaming. "Nobody there has lost a dog."

"Well, I hate to say it," Dr. Horst said, "but this little girl could have been abandoned."

"What?" Fin asked with a shocked tone, looking down at the dog. He seemed offended at the thought.

"People get a puppy," Dr. Horst said, "and it's so cute. But then it starts growing and becomes more of a hassle than they bargained for." He looked down at the dog. "This one won't get any bigger than this, but still she might have turned out to be more responsibility than they had planned on.

15

"So they go for a drive, find a remote road that's near some houses. Surely somebody there will take her in. They put her out and let her sniff around, and while she's distracted, they drive away."

"People do that?" Fin asked.

"I'm afraid it happens more often than you'd think. Happens with cats, too. With cats, though, they're already a little wild and independent, so they can adapt. Feral cats are all around, even in the city. Dogs, I'm afraid, usually don't adapt as easily."

Fin looked down at the dog again.

"Do you have any dogs?" Dr. Horst asked.

"No," Fin replied. "I've never had a dog. My mom had a cat when I was growing up, but I guess they weren't dog people."

"Well, looks like this little girl could use a home."

§

A few hundred dollars later, Fin arrived back home with the dog. She was wearing her new collar and leash, which he had purchased at a pet supplies store, along with numerous other things Fin needed to care for her.

After carrying the food, dishes, brush, beds and assorted chew toys in from his car, he pulled off his sunglasses feeling grateful again for being in the relative darkness of his home, away from the glare.

Having missed the nap that he had planned on after his walk, Fin was even more tired, so he plopped one of the dog beds on the floor in front of the sofa in his living room. The dog sniffed at it curiously, but when Fin patted the interior padding of the bed, she stepped into it, turned a couple of circles and lay down.

Time for Fin to do the same. Minus the circles.

§

Fin looked around at the forest. Something was wrong, but he didn't know what it was. He heard a strange sound, and it wasn't the snow squinching under his feet. In fact, he was surprised to see that the snow was gone. That wasn't entirely uncommon on the Front Range. They could get quite a bit of snow, then it warms up, the sun comes out, and the snow melts quickly.

This seemed especially quick, though.

He heard the sound again. It sounded almost like static, like a random crackling or hissing sound. He couldn't see what could be causing it.

Then, he noticed that the ground moved. Confused, he scrunched up his face and bent down to take a closer look. That's when he saw that it wasn't the ground that was moving, but all the spiders on it. And they were moving toward him.

He stepped back and heard a collective crunch under his foot. Looking around, he could see that the spiders were all around him. He was surrounded!

There were all kinds. Little brown recluses and black widows, big wolf spiders, and various kinds in between. Some were poisonous, most were harmless, but in this abundance, and apparent coordinated aggression, they all terrified him.

He frantically looked around for any place where the ground was not moving, but to no avail. It was all moving in his direction.

He started running toward his house, crunching several spiders with each step, but that's when he felt the movement on his legs under his pants. He reached down to swat the area where he felt the movement, and ended up swatting several spiders that were on the outside of his pant leg as well.

"Shit! Shit! Shit!" he exclaimed, looking at the twitching legs stuck to his hand.

Then he felt the prick on his leg. That was followed by another one, then one on his other leg.

He looked down and saw that his body was swarming with spiders, crawling up toward his face, or looking for openings in his clothing. Gasping for breath, he frantically swiped at them, brushing some off, but feeling the bites of others that managed to cling to his hand.

As the bites on his legs and hand became more frequent, he panicked and started pulling his clothes off. Fortunately, that knocked a lot of the spiders off of him that were clinging to his shirt and pants. Unfortunately, it further angered those that were still clinging to his legs.

His body was blazing with burning, itching spider bites. As he looked down at his body, he could see the red welts swelling, his body becoming distorted by the injected poison, the pain becoming more acute every second. He started shaking as the neurotoxins started affecting his nervous system, and he knew he wouldn't last much longer.

Overwhelmed, now, by the sheer number of the spiders biting him, Fin's strength was giving out, and he couldn't hold himself up any longer. He fell onto the ground, and the last thing he remembered was the darkness covering his eyes as the spiders swarmed over his face.

§

"Fuck!" Fin exclaimed as he sat up on the sofa. Panting for breath, he looked around and was relieved to see his living room. And he saw the little dog looking up at him. She had been startled by his sudden movement and outcry.

"Sorry," he said as he reached down to pet her.

He swung around and put his feet down on the floor, still shuddering from the dream. He felt a hair move against his pants, and he swatted at it, deep, hard goosebumps raising all over his body.

He took a deep breath and blew it out. The tension wouldn't go away. He looked down at the little dog, still watching him curiously, and Fin felt the sudden urge to hold her. He reached down and picked her up, taking comfort in her warm, fluffy little body.

"So," he said after he finally started to calm down, "what should I call you?" Happy to have something to focus on, he pondered for a few seconds. "You're the perfect size and temperament for an ironic name like Bruiser or Goliath. Or Cujo! That would be cool. But it turns out you're a girl."

Looking very much like an adorable stuffed toy, the dog snuggled against him, looking up at him, tilting her head as he addressed her.

"You're such a little teddy bear," Fin said, finally able to manage a smile. "I should call you Ursa Minor." Suddenly, his mind veered away from the Little Dipper as another thought occurred to him. "Ursula. Your name is Ursula."

## 2

Suzy Quinn surveyed the work that had been done in her dining room that day. She had mixed feelings about it, but her ambivalence had nothing to do with the quality of the work. Brian, the building contractor that she had hired was doing a good job. The other rooms that they had already completed were beautiful. And with the dining room, even at this stage, Suzy could see the room shaping up toward her goal.

"What are you looking so pensive about?" Rachel asked as she came in from the kitchen, handing Suzy one of the glasses of Cabernet she carried.

"Oh, you know," Suzy sighed, "just the history."

"Hmm," Rachel nodded. Rachel was an old friend who knew Suzy's history. She didn't require an explanation beyond that, but Suzy expounded.

"This was one of the first rooms I saw in this house in its original form. When Fiona was having dinner with Robert Drummond in 1827, I was there." She pointed to a location in the room where her table and chairs used to stand, but was now empty. Even the carpet had been removed, in anticipation of the wide plank flooring that was going to be installed.

"God, that's so creepy!" Rachel said with a shiver. Suzy looked at her and smiled wistfully.

"I know. I used to think so, too. But I've been lucky. I ended up getting close to the people I interacted with, so I'm pretty much cool with it."

"Ghosts, you mean. They *used* to be people. Now they're creepy ghosts."

"Okay," Suzy conceded, "some of them were creepy."

"Have you made any more contacts?" Rachel asked.

"No," Suzy shook her head, "not since Colorado. I don't have any more ghosts here, and I never go anywhere. How would I make any more contact?"

"I don't know," Rachel shrugged. "I guess I just keep hoping that maybe Mark or Emma . . ."

That remark brought Suzy's mood back, and she turned to look at the dining room again.

"Mark was so proud of that crown molding." She looked at the strips around the ceiling where the molding had been ripped out, now showing only bare sheetrock and gaping nail holes.

"I know, honey," Rachel said sympathetically. "But just remember how excited you were after you saw this house in those episodes with Fiona. Mark did a great job, and it was beautiful. It served its purpose very well for several years. But, as it turns out, it wasn't authentic to the original house." Rachel looked candidly at her. "That's what you're wanting, right?"

"Yes, that's right," Suzy admitted.

She showed the hint of a smile as the reminder of those episodes brought back that excitement. Seeing historical settings from the point of view of the ghosts she interacted with was fascinating. She had developed her SpiritSense to the point of, not only being able to receive visions from spirits, but to even have some influence over the spirits themselves, to help them move on. SpiritSense was a term that Lilith, her advisor in all things ghostly, had applied to Suzy.

But for Suzy, she had especially loved seeing her own house when it was only about forty years old. Over two hundred years old now, her family's sprawling estate in Marblehead, Massachusetts bore little resemblance to the little Scottish castle that her ancestor Phillip Drummond had built in the late eighteenth century. The castle was still there, but it had been added on to at various times with, apparently, no thought given to adhering to a cohesive design.

That, however, wasn't what prompted Suzy to undertake a renovation. Or, rather, it wasn't her primary motivation. If there was anybody in the world who could become her companion in the next chapter of her life, she knew it would be Fin MacKinley. But try as she might, Suzy hadn't been able to fully commit to Fin the way she knew he hoped she would.

She wanted it, too. But Mark was everywhere in the house. Despite the absence of his actual spirit, he haunted Suzy. In nearly every corner of the house, every room bore a memory of him. Or of Emma.

Mark was the one thing holding her back from committing herself fully to Fin. That had been the main reason she had set the goal of remodeling her house. The vision of Fiona simply provided the style.

She felt bad about putting Fin off about Christmas. He really wanted to spend it with her, but Brian's schedule was such that he was available for interior work right up to Christmas and immediately after. She thought it was important enough that she wanted to make use of his availability. She still loved Mark and Emma, but she needed to be able to have a life which didn't involve them pulling her into the past with them. Suzy knew it wasn't their fault, but the pull was very real. They were still there.

But they had been dead for over three years. In those three years, Suzy had resisted changing anything. Emma's room remained exactly the same as it had been on that cold October day. The decorating that Suzy and Mark had done remained unchanged since the day Mark and Emma disappeared into the harbor.

Feeling the return of her guilt, Suzy resisted. She knew it wasn't constructive, so she tried to push the memory back, calling Fin to mind once more.

"You deserve to be able to enjoy your life again," Rachel said, as if she could see Suzy's dark thoughts.

"Get out of my head, Rachel," Suzy said, putting her arm around her friend. "*I'm* supposed to be the psychic here. You're my loyal sidekick."

"No, I'm the perceptive friend who's around to offer sage advice at critical moments."

"You don't want to be my sidekick?"

"You already have a sidekick," Rachel said, inclining her forehead against Suzy's. "He's in Colorado."

§

Suzy rinsed out the wine glasses and placed them in the dishwasher. She felt better now. Rachel always seemed to know the right thing to say. She thought for a moment about Rachel's comment about being her wise friend.

Which reminded her of her following comment about Fin being her sidekick. She started looking around for her phone. She found it on the hall table, next to her keys, near the front door.

She saw that Fin had sent her a text message earlier in the day. She had been so distracted all day long that she hadn't noticed. Suzy opened up her messaging app and read his message.

"Hey Suzy, I finished it. It's on its way to my editor."

She smiled. Fin had started the novel about nine months before, when Suzy was visiting him in Colorado. He had decided to turn their experience with a ghost she met out there in Silver Plume into a novel.

"Congratulations!" she replied. "What's next?" She looked at the walnut grandfather clock, which really had been her grandfather's. It was nearly nine-thirty. It was two hours earlier in Colorado, though, so Fin's reply came immediately.

"Nothing for now. Just relaxing with my dog."

Suzy frowned and touched the telephone receiver icon at the top of the messaging app. Fin answered right away.

"You got a dog?" Suzy asked before Fin had even completed saying hello.

"I found her today," Fin replied. "I went for a walk after I sent off the manuscript. You know that trail behind my house, the one that goes up into the forest?"

Suzy knew it well. She had walked the trail with Fin last April. It wasn't so much the walk that she remembered

23

fondly, but the steamy shower and lovemaking episode that had immediately followed it.

"I seem to recall something about that, yeah."

"She was tangled up in some bramble at the base of a tree. She's a Pomeranian. Cutest little thing. She looks like a teddy bear."

Suzy's phone dinged in her ear. She looked at it and saw the photo that Fin had just sent her.

"Oh my god," Suzy said, temporarily losing hold of her smartass persona, "she's adorable. Wait, though, you said you just found her? What if somebody claims her?"

"She was abandoned. You remember how small and remote my neighborhood is. I checked around. Nobody lost her, so Ursula's mine."

"Ursula?" Suzy replied, hoping that her raised eyebrows transmitted, somehow, through her tone of voice. "You know, most people give a cute dog a cute name."

"Well, Suzy Q, I'm sure you must know by now that I'm not most people. Besides, there's a nerd factor involved in her name."

"A nerd factor?"

"Absolutely. Ursula K. Le Guin was one of my favorite authors. She died a couple of years ago. And, as if that wasn't reason enough, Ursula means 'Little Bear.' Just look at this little thing. It's a perfect fit!"

"I suppose you're right," Suzy said with a smile at Fin's palpable excitement. The smile *did* transmit through her voice. "Ursula it is, then."

"So, how are you?" Fin asked "I haven't talked to you in a couple of days."

"I'm fine. How about you?"

"I'm good. Felt the beginnings of a migraine this morning when I was out on my walk. But my magic nose spray and Ursula have made it all better. Yes she has. Yes she has."

Suzy rolled her eyes as she pictured Fin baby-talking to Ursula.

"Maybe I should leave you two alone," she said. "You don't need a third wheel."

"No, I love you, babe." Fin replied, donning his normal voice again. "I'll *always* need you." The sound of his voice, and especially the thought expressed, warmed her heart.

# 3

With a few exceptions, Fin wasn't accustomed to hearing strange sounds in his house during the night. So, when he woke up in the middle of the night, he was startled to hear the noises. He was even more startled to discover the source.

He looked down at the corner formed by his wall and his dresser, where he had placed one of the little beds he had gotten for Ursula. Illuminated by light shining through the clerestory window and French doors in his bedroom, the little dog was growling and snarling at him.

"Ursula, what is it, girl?" He almost laughed when he realized that, aside from the name, he had uttered the clichéd line from the old Lassie show. If he hadn't been so freaked out, he might have asked if Timmy had fallen in the well. Ursula's behavior, though, was no laughing matter. She was acting rabid, crazed, and Fin felt goosebumps raise on his arms as he tried to think of what would cause such a reaction from the dog.

He sat up in bed, and Ursula stood up, her snarling, barking and snapping increasing as if Fin was a threat to her. Suddenly, she leapt on his lap, her teeth bared, and Fin fell back, stunned by the little dog's reaction.

"Ursula, it's okay," he said breathlessly, trying to push her away, but suddenly, she seemed to have grown. The little Pomeranian was as big and threatening as Cujo, and he was having a hard time keeping her from grabbing him by the throat. Strings of spittle were flying as she repeatedly lunged at him, her teeth snapping audibly inches from his face.

Her barking and snarling increased in pitch and intensity as she leapt up and landed with a thud on Fin's chest, crushing the breath from his lungs. He screamed as he frantically pushed her away, but her teeth repeatedly ripped and slashed at his arms, the blood spraying and gushing down, puddling on his chest and running off his shoulders, saturating his bed.

Fin could feel his strength giving out, and he knew the end was near. Whimpering in terror, he tried in vain to keep the dog's jaws from his throat, but he knew he couldn't hold her off any longer.

Suddenly, she was gone. Fin, gasping for breath, was almost as startled, now, by the eerie silence in his room. He wearily held his arms up in front of him. In the dim light from the window, he could see that his arms were fine. The ribbons of flesh were miraculously healed, the dark stains of blood were gone.

He lifted his head, feeling dizzy from the adrenaline coursing through his veins, and he fearfully looked down toward Ursula's bed. The dog was there, looking up at him, her little body quivering in fear.

§

Fin, his hands still shaking, poured coffee into his mug. Then, he went to the sink and picked up the rag to mop up the drops of coffee he spilled. He sighed and picked up his mug with both hands, looking out the window at the fenced-in back yard. It was still dark, but he had the light over his deck turned on. Ursula was making tracks through the four-inch blanket of snow, expanding from the explorations she had begun the day before.

Fin couldn't get that terrifying scene out of his head. His first thought was that, like the spiders, it had been a very realistic dream. But he was certain that he had been awake. There was no moment he could point to as a time when he could have awakened from the dream. The logical point would be when the beast vanished and Fin's wounds instantly healed, but there wasn't a transition from asleep to awake. He was sure he was conscious before that.

Then, despite how silly the idea initially seemed to him, he wondered if Ursula could be a ghost, some kind of supernatural animalian being that takes on a different form depending on its mood. It wouldn't be the first time he had brought a supernatural being into his house.

But then he realized that this really was a silly idea. He had taken the dog to the vet, had her examined by a doctor who physically poked and prodded her. Ursula wasn't a ghost.

The next thought that occurred to him, though, made his stomach clench, because he realized it was more likely. It involved the aforementioned uninvited guest that had appeared in his home last April, after he and Suzy had come back from Silver Plume. Having brought back a souvenir of their trip, they had also brought a ghost that was connected to it. Could Ursula have a ghost attached to her, or worse, be possessed by some kind of evil spirit?

He raised his mug to his lips to take a sip of coffee just as a violent shiver racked his body. He sighed again as he ripped a paper towel off the roll and wiped his face and dabbed at the wet spots on his shirt.

He saw Ursula come running up the steps toward the sliding glass door in his kitchen, plumes of snow flying as she plowed through it. Fin, his body still tense, slid the door open and let her in. Fin watched her warily as she shook, snow flying from her fur. Then, she looked up at him to see where he was going to go. When he stayed there, she curled up on the rug.

Suzy had told him back in April that everybody has the latent ability to make contact with spirits. Whether or not that ability is developed depends on how open-minded and accepting the individual is of the whole concept. Fin had expressed a less-than-thrilled reaction to the news.

As it turned out, apparently, acceptance wasn't as great a factor as open-mindedness, because at the end of their adventure in Silver Plume, he had indeed made contact with the ghosts, to his chagrin. He was creeped out by Suzy's ability to basically relive the ghost's life, and it wasn't an ability that he wanted for himself.

He had always been fascinated by the idea of time travel, so that part of it wasn't an issue. He had, in fact, become a commercially successful author based on his novels that employed time travel as a plot device. But in Suzy's case, the fact that it was done through a dead person made Fin shudder. The thought that he might have one in his house again, without Suzy's expertise and support, terrified him.

He looked down at the fluffy little dog curled up on his rug, sleeping peacefully. "She's so adorable," Fin thought. "No way she's the conduit to a demonic entity."

He knelt down beside her and scratched her ear.

§

"Lilith said that it *is* possible," Suzy told him.

Lilith, the sweet little old ghost expert in Marblehead, was the one that Suzy had consulted on numerous occasions. Fin had called Suzy to tell her about his frightening encounter with Ursula's alter ego, and to get feedback on his conjecture. Now, an hour or so later, she had called back.

"Spirits have been known to attach themselves to living creatures, although it's pretty rare with so-called lower animals. But even from a Christian background, there's the story of Jesus casting demons out of a man. From him, they went into a herd of swine and drove them all over a cliff. So, it's not unheard of."

"Shit," Fin said under his breath.

"What are you going to do?"

"I have no idea. What do you suggest? Did Lilith have any thoughts on that?"

"She did," Suzy replied. "A few of them, in fact, ranging from off-the-wall to downright weird, depending on your belief system, including engaging a priest to perform an exorcism. But I know you don't come from a Catholic background, and even if you did, I don't know if a priest would be willing to perform an exorcism on a dog."

Fin sighed, looking at Ursula's happy little face looking up at him.

"Have you made any kind of contact other than the experience during the night?" Suzy asked. "Have you felt a presence, heard a voice, felt a prickling at the back of your neck? Anything?"

"No," Fin replied, "nothing at all. Aside from that attack, it's been perfectly normal around here. Quiet and routine, just the way I like it."

"Have you brought anything else into your home recently, other than the dog?"

"Just the stuff I bought *for* the dog. Brand new, from the pet supplies store."

There was a long pause, during which Fin imagined that Suzy was probably considering him a basket case.

"Are you absolutely certain you couldn't have dreamed it?"

"Well, after this process of elimination, no, I can't say without a doubt that it wasn't a dream." Fin took a long, shuddering breath and exhaled it. "It sure didn't seem like one, though."

## 4

After visiting with Fin for a while, and comforting him after his scare, Suzy touched the disconnect button on her phone and slipped it into the pocket of her sweater. Their discussion had convinced her that it could only be a dream, and Fin was feeling better.

She was standing in her dining room again. Brian, the contractor, and his partner were due to arrive in a few minutes, to continue their work.

Last night, standing in this room, Rachel had sparked the memory of Suzy's episode with her ancestress, Fiona, having dinner here back in 1827. This morning, though, a different memory came to mind, as she saw a gouge in the sheetrock. It had been covered by the crown molding, but was now uncovered, bringing the memory back.

Mark had just sold his latest venture and had made a tidy profit. Entrepreneurial success had apparently been written into his DNA, and Suzy marveled at the ease with which he slipped into a new business idea, and usually made a success of it.

This one involved a cell phone or computer app that he had created. Aimed at children, it had the lofty goal of making them *want* to do mundane things that parents often had to resort to threats and bribery to accomplish. Using fun characters that the kids could build for themselves, the app employed a system whereby children could earn points and apply rewards to their beloved characters whenever they accomplished any of the chores.

The company that Mark had created was purchased by a toothpaste company that had the commendable goal of getting kids to brush their teeth for at least two minutes. Of course, their ultimate goal was to sell more toothpaste.

He had a few ideas for his next venture, but until he decided on one, he and Suzy were working on remodeling the dining room. They were installing the crown molding that she had mentioned to Rachel the night before. Suzy didn't know anything about construction, but Mark did. Of course. One of his earlier jobs had involved various phases of construction, so Suzy was following his lead.

It was the first summer after they were married. It was warm and Mark had taken his shirt off. Suzy found herself frequently stealing glances at him.

Standing on an old wooden ladder that she had pulled from the tool shed, Suzy was holding one end of a piece of molding while Mark countersunk a nail in the other end. He slipped his hammer into its loop on his tool belt and climbed down his newer fiberglass ladder.

"You're looking pretty sexy there, mister," Suzy said. Mark looked up at her and wiggled his eyebrows at her. He swished his hips in a circular motion, causing his hammer and other tools to swing around in an exaggerated arc.

To Suzy, the sight was a strange combination of sexy and ridiculous. She snickered, but her amusement abruptly stopped when she heard a crack and felt the step on her old ladder giving way. She scrambled to grab the top of the ladder, letting go of the molding, but her fingernails raked across the rough, splintering top cap before she could get a grip on it.

She squealed briefly until she felt Mark's arms catch her.

"Easy, miss," he said, quoting *Superman*, "I've got you."

Suzy gasped, catching her breath, before she continued the quote.

"You've got me? Who's got you?"

Mark smiled and put her down on her feet. They looked at the molding that she had been holding, lying on the floor now. It had broken from the attached end, leaving a deep gouge in the sheetrock.

"Oh, Mark," Suzy groaned.

"No problem," Mark said, as he picked up the molding and cut the jagged end off at a 45 degree angle with his miter saw. Prying off the broken end that he had nailed, they started the process all over again, with Suzy standing on Mark's ladder, and Mark standing on a chair.

Suzy sighed as she remembered that day.

"'Till death do you part' is a crock," she said. Then, she shook her head. "Poor Fin."

The doorbell rang, and she turned to let Brian in.

# 5

I t was a Currier and Ives kind of morning. Cold and overcast, the sharply-angled and filtered sunlight cast an almost sepia tint on the snow and the houses. Being a lover of history, Fin especially appreciated the old-timey look that his neighborhood wore.

*Brittle, emaciated fingers of frigid sunlight claw in vain through somber clouds.*

Fin liked that sentence that crept into his mind, and he woke up his phone so he could record it. He might be able to use it in a book at some point. He looked back out at the idyllic setting.

It was almost enough to take his mind off the terror he had experienced a few hours ago.

Even with the clouds, though, it was still intensely bright. Feeling another twinge behind his eye, Fin closed the blinds and turned from the window. Ursula looked up at him from her bed. Fin had gotten her three beds, one for the three rooms he occupied most, his bedroom, his family room and his library. She followed him wherever he went in the house, and if she had a bed there, that's where she settled until he moved again.

He sat down at his desk and looked at his computer. It always felt strange in that limbo zone between books. He felt like he should be doing something, but he didn't know what. He had a few vague ideas for new books, but nothing really fleshed out into an actual story.

Ursula laid her head back down, and the movement caught Fin's eye. He looked at her for a few moments, feeling the return of that cold, creepy feeling that had settled in his chest all morning.

He remembered recalling Cujo during his dream of the attack. He was reminded that Stephen King had been inspired by a near attack that happened to him. Fin realized that his own experience could provide similar inspiration.

Having just written a ghost story, the supernatural was on Fin's mind, especially after considering the possibility that morning of Ursula being a ghost, or of being possessed by one. He hated the fact that he felt distanced now from the little dog because of the dream, but he hoped that time would make the terror of the dream gradually fade from his memory.

That twinge behind his eye was still nagging him. He didn't want it to turn into an actual migraine. Better have another squirt of the nose spray.

§

Once he had nipped the migraine in the bud, the ideas flowed. It was the kind of day where he forgot to eat. The hunger pangs weren't enough to draw him away from his computer. It was Ursula who finally pulled his attention away from the burgeoning outline.

It was dark outside when he had gotten up to feed her and let her out, scarfing down some leftovers from the fridge. But even then, his head was still in the story that he was building. Inspired in part by his dream early this morning, and partly by an earlier ghostly experience, with Suzy, of course, the story was about a dog that had been possessed by the spirit of an evil medicine man.

He admitted to himself that, distilled down to a single sentence like that, it sounded rather silly, but likely most of Stephen King's stories probably would, too. Still, from that basic idea, he was crafting a story that, he thought, would have best-seller potential.

It would take a fair amount of fleshing out, but his rough outline was building very nicely. He liked the story that was taking shape.

Considering how early he had gotten up that morning, it wasn't very late when fatigue pulled on the reins and said, 'no more!' After letting Ursula out one more time, he saved his file and climbed the stairs, the little dog scampering after him.

"No attacks tonight, okay?" Fin said to Ursula. She plopped down in her bed and looked up at him, tilting her head to the side. Her reddish-gold fur almost glowing in the warm light of Fin's bedside lamp, she looked as if she had a flaming mane around her head. "Look at you," Fin smiled, "you're on fire. Well, you've certainly filled this place with warmth, anyway. Such a pretty little thing. How could anybody give you up?"

§

Fin groggily opened his eyes when he heard a loud popping sound. His bedroom was ablaze, flames writhing up the walls, the room awash in fiery gold. The ceiling was alive with flames rippling across it, flames that hadn't yet found a handhold, but were scrambling for one.

Suddenly, he was wide awake. He threw the covers off of him and jumped out of bed. He snatched up Ursula and dashed out the door, trying to dodge the flames.

The hallway was even more engulfed than his bedroom had been. The thought that flashed through his mind was that the lights on the little Christmas tree in his library must have shorted out. The thought was brief, though. He had to get out. As he rushed toward the stairs, the ceiling collapsed, flaming rafters and sheetrock raining down around him.

The heat was stifling, and he struggled to take a breath, feeling the heat burn down his throat with each inhalation. The stairway was a little more open, and he managed to get down the stairs without incident.

The first floor, though, was a confusing maelstrom of smoke and heat. There was nothing recognizable as he picked his way through the flames and smoldering rubble. Holding Ursula close to him, he held his other hand up in front of him to shield his face. Based on the direction he was facing when he reached the bottom of the stairs, he knew, roughly, where the front door was, but there was a deadly obstacle course in between.

Picking his way through the inferno, he struggled not to panic, but he could feel the adrenalin coursing through his veins. He could feel the hair on his legs being singed, his skin crisping in the heat. The toxic smoke filled his lungs, and he knew it wouldn't be very long before he would succumb to the effects.

Finally, he reached the front door. As he hyperventilated, he tried to turn the deadbolt, burning his fingers in the process. Knowing he was about to die literally within inches of safety, the tears streamed down his cheeks as he finally got the knob turned, and he yanked the door open.

He ran out into his front yard, the welcome darkness of night enveloping him, as he gulped great breaths of clean, fresh air. The freezing air was a shock to his body, but the snow was refreshingly cold around his bare feet. He could almost hear the steam as the snow around his legs rapidly transitioned from solid to gaseous form. He turned around, wishing he had thought to grab his phone. He needed to call the fire department.

Except that his house was dark. Standing in the snow in his underwear, Fin looked at the house, the windows dark and cavernous looking back at him, mocking him. Ursula looked up at him, but he avoided her eyes.

As he felt the cold start settling into his body, he looked around, hoping none of the neighbors were up to see this. Embarrassed, he started trudging back toward the front door.

§

Fin sat in his library staring down into the blackness of his third cup of coffee, while happy holiday music wafted around him. He had asked Alexa to play Celtic Christmas music, thinking that it might lift his spirits, but the exuberance of David Arkenstone's *Christmas Day in the Morning* was lost on him.

He looked at the dark Christmas tree in the corner. Remembering the suspected cause of the non-existent fire, he couldn't bring himself to keep the lights on. He had un-plugged it.

He lifted his cup and took a sip, looking at Ursula as he did. The little dog lay in her bed, dozing occasionally, but looking up at Fin whenever he moved. Fin couldn't determine if she was wondering what the hell she had gotten herself into with him, or if she was plotting her next attack.

He hadn't noticed what time this particular nightmare had happened, but at least a couple of hours had passed and it was still dark outside. He still couldn't determine if it even was a nightmare, or if there was something more nefarious at play. It had been so real! He shuddered as he remembered how close death had seemed.

After the second night in a row of this, it was going to be a rough day. He could feel a headache coming on.

# 6

Your Christmas tree looks a little anemic," Rachel commented. She was studying the tree in the corner of Suzy's living room, next to the windows looking out on the harbor between her home on Marblehead Neck and mainland Marblehead. The tree was bare except for a few ornaments. It looked as if Suzy had started decorating it, but lost interest partway through. Suzy looked at it from her usual place on the sofa and agreed.

"I know. I just haven't done much for Christmas in the last few years."

"Why not?" Rachel asked, though she already knew the answer.

"Christmas is for kids, for families. I don't have anybody."

"What am I, chopped livah?" Rachel chided with a forced New York accent, though it wasn't very convincing. Suzy was much better with accents.

"You know what I mean. I don't have any family."

"It's also for friends, you know," Rachel protested. "I don't have any family around here, either, but I still enjoy getting together with my friends for the holidays. Even you!" she added acerbically.

"I just don't see the point," Suzy replied in a flat tone. Rachel knew her friend was having a hard time when she passed up an opportunity to make a smartass response.

"Why did you put the tree up at all?"

Suzy looked at it for a few moments, then sighed.

"Habit," she shrugged. "Mark and I always made a production out of setting up and decorating the tree. I guess I just wanted to see if I could do it on my own. I mean, of course I *can*." Suzy looked at it again and raised her eyebrows. "But from the looks of it, maybe I shouldn't." She gave the first expression approximating a smile that Rachel had seen since she had arrived that evening.

"Thank you for coming over again," Suzy said, looking at her friend. "You really didn't have to."

"I don't want you to be alone," Rachel replied simply.

"Well, what about you? You're still relatively young and not entirely unpleasant to look at." Rachel smiled. There was the Suzy she knew. "You should be out there dating. I don't want you to be alone, either."

"I'm not alone. I'm with you."

Suzy smiled and rested her hand on Rachel's shoulder. She took a sip of her tea. It was lukewarm now, but she didn't care.

§

After Rachel left, Suzy wandered back over toward the Christmas tree. It really *was* anemic. There were only three ornaments hanging on it. The last one she had hung was a delicate-looking snowflake. It was one that Mark had bought on a weekend getaway they had taken their first Christmas together.

Mark had booked a couple of nights in a charming little B&B in the Berkshires. It was truly a beautiful old-fashioned White Christmas.

The owners of the B&B were a funny older couple, Joe and Anita Grundwald. Joe was a quiet one, but Anita was, in Mark's words, 'a tough old broad.' Mark, being more of an extrovert than Suzy, had struck up several conversations with them. During the course of these conversations, they had learned all about the Grundwalds' history. They also learned about their two sons who, while growing up, often fought with each other, actual knock-down-drag-out punchfests, apparently, purely for entertainment.

"It was the worst in the wintertime," Anita had said. "Warmer seasons, I could just push 'em out the door and let 'em slug it out in the yard. But in the winter, I couldn't do that and still be a good mom. So they'd start walloping on each other. I'd tell 'em, 'Take it down to the basement. Call me if there's blood.'"

At breakfast their first morning, Suzy and Mark had a small table to themselves. Suzy had leaned forward and whispered to Mark that she noticed that the walls were quite thin, that she had been able to hear others moving around.

"So if we have sex here," she whispered, "mum's the word."

Mark started panting.

"Mum, mum, mum," he said, repeating the word over and over with each exhalation, each repetition rising a little in volume, as if approaching a passionate and embarrassingly noisy orgasm.

Suzy sputtered, trying to hold back the laughter, but not doing a very good job of it. At the same time, she grabbed Mark's hand, to get him to stop, which he did. He just sat back in his chair, watching as she gradually brought the hysteria under control, and he smiled at her.

"I love that sound," he said. Suzy looked self-consciously at the other guests, hoping they hadn't heard what had caused her outburst.

"What sound?" Suzy asked quietly, wiping the tears from her eyes with her napkin. "The sound of your freakin' mumgasm?"

"Your laughter," Mark replied. "That's absolutely the sweetest sound in the world to me."

Suzy's eyes filled with tears again, but not from laughter.

§

After the memory associated with that snowflake ornament, Suzy hadn't been able to continue decorating the tree. She decided she needed to direct her thoughts outside herself, and she realized she hadn't had any contact with Fin again that day. Having been distracted, like the day before, with the remodeling work, and then with Rachel, she hadn't noticed that Fin had tried to contact her three times.

She sighed when it occurred to her that she hadn't made herself available to him in this difficult time, with his fear of another haunting. It was a difficult time for Suzy, too, but she hadn't shared with Fin what she was doing. He had no idea of the solemn introspection that she was going through.

She touched Fin's number to call him back.

'm sorry I've been such a bad girlfriend," Suzy said as soon as Fin answered his phone.

"You're not a bad girlfriend," Fin replied wearily. "You're the best."

"I haven't been here for you."

"It's okay. You have a life. You can't be here for me all the time. Not yet, anyway," Fin added with a bit of a smile. It was all he could muster at the time.

"What's up?" Suzy asked, hesitant to respond to the latter insinuation.

"It happened again."

"You dreamed about Ursula attacking you again?"

"No, this time it was a fire."

He related in harrowing detail the dream or vision or whatever it was. Suzy was quiet for a few moments after he finished.

"You've never experienced anything like this before?" she finally asked.

"No."

"And you still haven't had any other contact from a ghost, or any kind of spirit?"

"No."

"Well, Fin," Suzy sighed, "I don't know what it could be. It does sound like it could be a haunting, but I can't figure out what could be causing it. Unless there really is a ghost connected to Ursula."

Fin looked down at the dog sleeping in her bed. Having already grown attached to her, he hated to think of her being the cause of his recent troubles.

"So, what are you going to do?" Suzy asked.

"I'm probably going to go to bed as soon as we hang up. Then, assuming I survive the night, tomorrow I'll start looking for a good local canine exorcist."

"Hmm," Suzy replied ambiguously. "Good luck."

"Thanks. So," he said, trying to sound perky, in an attempt to change the subject, "I feel like I've been hogging the limelight recently. What have you been up to lately?"

There was a long pause. Fin was just about to ask if Suzy had heard his question when she finally responded.

"I'm having my home remodeled."

"Oh my god, Suzy!" Fin said, his voice taking on a sympathetic tone. "That's huge. Are you okay?"

"It's definitely stirring up some memories, but yes, I'm fine."

"Sounds like I've been a bad boyfriend. I had no idea you were going through that."

"Why don't we call it even, vow to work on it, and not mention it again?" Suzy said.

"It's a deal," Fin smiled. "So, what are you doing to your home?"

"I'm having it restored to a style similar to when Fiona was there."

"Very cool. I guess you had a lot of reference material to draw from."

"Not as much as you might think," Suzy said, her voice sounding a little more animated.

"Really? But I thought you saw several episodes in that house when Fiona lived there."

"I did, but I had no control over where Fiona looked. Seeing it through her eyes, I saw what she saw. At those times, I wasn't me, I was Fiona. I had no influence over her, I was just seeing her memories of things that had already happened."

"Things that happened in that house."

"Right, but I couldn't look around to see details. If the episode I saw took place after she had first seen a particular room, and she wasn't focusing on the room itself, then I couldn't make her turn her head so I could see something specific. The décor was just peripheral."

"Of course."

"But, I remember details that I did directly see, and I've been able to recall a little more through meditation. So, making use of what I have, I've consulted with Jay and a few other historians at the local museum, and perused numerous books and other references. When it's done, I think it's going to be very faithful to the time."

"But a difficult process," Fin said understandingly.

"It is, but I think it'll be worth it in the end."

§

Fin fell asleep within seconds of crawling into bed. His sleep was deep and dreamless, and he woke up feeling more refreshed than he had in a while.

He looked down toward Ursula's bed, but it was empty. Pushing himself up on his elbow, he saw her, standing up against the side of his bed, her tongue lolling out of her mouth, her curled tail wagging furiously. Fin reached down and lifted her up on the bed with him, and she immediately curled up on his comforter against him.

"Don't get used to this," Fin said. "You're not going to start sleeping in my bed." His stern tone was belied by his adoring smile. "You probably need to go outside, don't you?" She lifted her head and looked at him, her face completely alert, as if she had already learned those words. "Okay, come on," he said as he picked her up and set her back down on the floor again.

He got out of bed, glad that today was already looking up.

Suzy stood in the doorway of Emma's room. She would have been twelve years old now. Her room had, aside from dusting and vacuuming, remained untouched since the day she died three years ago.

Suzy remembered the day they brought her home from the hospital. It was a warm spring morning in May. Emma had, apparently, been anxious to come out into the world. According to the doctor, she wasn't due until June, although Suzy had expected that she would come earlier. After they examined her, they found no health issues, and she was a healthy weight. The doctor was willing to admit that his calculation of the due date may have been a little off.

Emma's animated eagerness remained with her throughout her short life. She was eager to start school, eager for every holiday that came along, eager for every vacation they planned.

Eager to go out on the boat on a cold day in October, three years ago.

Suzy sighed and pulled the door closed.

*Your room won't be touched, baby.*

§

Brian and his partner, Mike, were busy working in the dining room. Brian had told her they were nearly finished, and would soon be ready to move to the next room. That would be the family room.

She had already moved a number of things out of there, in anticipation of their work. All the furniture had either been moved into a different room, or pushed into the center of the family room and covered with drop cloths. The urns holding Mark and Emma's ashes had been moved from the mantel of the fireplace, and were safely in a box in Suzy's bedroom. Other things had been cleared out, as well. She was using the time now to go through some things that were in a built-in cabinet, putting the things she wanted to keep in a box, and throwing out the things she knew she didn't need.

Suzy frowned, looking down at the movie ticket stubs she held in her hand, trying to decide which category they belonged in.

*Back to the Future*, 20th Anniversary. Mark knew that she loved that series of movies. Suzy had been a little girl when the first movie was released, but her parents loved it, and they watched their VHS copy of it numerous times. So when a nearby theater was going to play the first in the trilogy on the twentieth anniversary of its release, Suzy snatched up a couple of tickets.

It turned out to be more than just a movie.

It seemed as if everything was going wrong that evening. Dinner was late. She had left Mark stirring the marinara sauce as she went upstairs to change. It was still cold when she came back down. She was certain that the burner had been up higher than "warm" when she left, but Mark assured her he hadn't touched it.

Then, Mark couldn't find the blazer he wanted to wear. Suzy insisted that he didn't need a jacket. It was July, for god's sakes! But he finally found it, and they were able to leave.

That wasn't the last of the problems, though. Mark turned right on Loring Avenue, north toward Salem, instead of left, toward the theater.

"What's wrong?" Suzy asked, starting to feel a little concerned. "This isn't like you. You always know exactly where to go."

"Sorry, babe," he replied, distracted, as he attempted to make a series of right turns to get back on track. Merging into traffic, they were finally heading southwest on Loring.

"You know I like to be there to see the previews."

"I know you do," he said. "I'll get you there."

The theater was already dark when they walked in. Suzy was annoyed that they had gotten there after the trailers had started. The theater was pretty full, but despite the darkness, Mark spotted a couple of empty seats and led the way. A teaser for a movie called *The Da Vinci Code* was playing, due out nearly a year later. They had just gotten sat down when he turned to her.

"Do you want anything to eat or drink?" he whispered. "Popcorn? Candy?"

"No, I'm fine," she replied, trying not to sound as irritated with him as she was feeling.

"Okay, I'll be back," he said as he climbed over her legs and the people next to her, back out to the aisle.

The next preview, *Pirates of the Caribbean: Dead Man's Chest*, looked pretty good. There were trailers for a new James Bond movie, a new *Mission: Impossible* movie and a new Superman movie, but Mark still wasn't back yet. What the hell was he doing? Suzy was starting to get a little miffed with him.

Then, the next preview started, and Suzy thought it seemed a little out of place. Theaters usually showed previews of movies of a similar genre, so trailers of other adventure movies, like the ones she had just seen, were expected. This one started out like a kind of corny domestic drama.

She recognized the area. There were scenes in various places around Marblehead, exterior shots of some of the very places that Suzy and Mark frequented, so she was attentive. But she didn't remember hearing about a movie being filmed nearby.

Then, she saw someone that looked a lot like Rachel. Suzy knew that Rachel had expressed a mild interest in movies in the past. But if she had gotten a part as an extra or something like that, Suzy was sure that she would have told her about it before now.

"She's my best friend," 'Rachel' said. It even sounded like her, too. "I care very much about her. You better make her happy!"

"I will," replied Mark. It really *was* Mark! "I promise you, I'll do everything in my power to make her happy."

Suzy kept watching as other people she knew appeared on the screen, talking about their friend. And Mark kept appearing there with them.

The scenes were building to an emotional climax, and she couldn't believe that Mark wasn't here to see this! Then, the music swelled, the visuals speeded up and intensified in brightness, and suddenly, they frenetically spiraled into a point of light in the middle of the screen and stopped. The screen was dark, and there was a moment of confused silence. Then, the lights came up.

And there was Mark standing at the front of the theater.

"Suzy," he said with a smile, "you don't have any idea how hard it was for me to make us late. You said yourself, this isn't like me. But I needed to get us here after the lights were out."

Suzy felt the person next to her bump against her shoulder. She turned and looked. It was Rachel. Suzy looked at her, her mouth hanging open, and she began to see other familiar faces around her, smiling at her.

"You know I love you," Mark continued, "and that I would do absolutely anything for you. Well, honey, the first thing I want to do is make an honest woman out of you. What do you say, Suzy? Will you marry me?"

Suzy had never cared for that expression, to 'make an honest woman out of her.' But having gotten caught up in the emotion that had built during the fake trailer, and now Mark's proposal, she decided it was an instance in which she should choose her battles. She loved Mark, and she couldn't think of anybody that she would rather spend the rest of her life with than him.

That figure of speech wasn't battle material.

"Yes," she nodded, with tears in her eyes.

The theater erupted in applause, even the majority who didn't know Suzy or Mark. She didn't know how he had finagled this with the theater, but knowing Mark, it probably hadn't been very difficult.

As Mark started running back up the aisle to their seats, Rachel threw her arms around Suzy and hugged her.

"I'm so happy for you both!" she said with tears in her eyes.

Mark climbed over the knees of the couple on the end of the row, whom Suzy didn't know, then Rachel's, and finally Suzy's. Suzy stood up and Mark kissed her, and there was a smattering of applause again. After a few moments, the lights went down in the theater and the Universal Pictures logo appeared on the screen.

Suzy sat down. Mark seemed bewildered for a moment, then sat down next to her.

"What are you doing?" he asked.

"The movie's starting," Suzy whispered in reply.

"Okay, but – I"

"Sshh."

"I thought you might want to go out and celebrate," Mark said in a whisper.

"I bought these tickets," Suzy explained, quite seriously, "I love this movie. I want to watch it!"

It was all Suzy could do to keep from jumping up and down and running out of the theater with Mark. But she had been on the receiving end of enough of his jokes that she decided that this was important. So they stayed and watched the movie.

After that start, and being the twentieth anniversary of the movie, the audience was kind of rowdy, almost as if it had been a midnight showing of *The Rocky Horror Picture Show*. They cheered when Marty and the DeLorean first reached eighty-eight miles per hour and escaped the Libyan terrorists. They booed when Biff was assaulting Lorraine, cheered again when George punched him out, and they applauded when Marty finished his rowdy version of *Johnny B. Goode*.

They did go out and celebrate, with Rachel and a few others, but only after the movie was over.

Looking down at the ticket stubs, she blinked back the tears.

*Dammit Mark!*

## 9

Fin was taking advantage of the clear head he had after a good night's sleep. He had forgotten his vow to Suzy the evening before about finding an exorcist. Instead, sitting at his computer, he had completed the outline for the new novel he had envisioned a couple of days ago, and now, he was starting on the actual writing.

Using his own experiences, it almost felt like cheating. But they say, 'write what you know,' so that's what he was doing. Combining details from his adventure with Suzy in Silver Plume back in April with recent events with Ursula, whether real or imagined, he was pleased with how the story was opening up.

Suzy had told him once that his books read like screenplays. She said that his scenes were described so well that they could be visualized as if the reader were watching a movie. Fin couldn't think of a nicer compliment that anyone could pay a writer.

After a few hours, he got up and walked around his library to stretch his legs. He opened the blinds, but the bright sunlight amplified by the snow on the ground was too painful, so he closed them again.

"God, I'm turning into a vampire," he said to Ursula, who was following him around. Ursula tilted her head at him, but didn't respond.

He realized that he was hungry, and he noticed that it was nearly one o'clock. He made a sandwich, and then sat back down at his computer to continue working.

§

It had been a productive day. Several pages into his new novel, Fin was happy with the way it was shaping up already.

He had taken Ursula out for a walk in the afternoon. The snow was melting under the bright sunshine, but there was still a lot of it around, so Fin made sure he was protected, with a wide-brimmed hat and dark sunglasses. Unfortunately, the sunglasses didn't cover the sides, or fully protect from the glare reflecting upwards, so he still felt the occasional stab from the blazing sunlight.

It was a relief to get back inside, and to get back to his book. Several hours later, after a brief chat with Suzy and a little more tapping at his computer, he climbed the stairs to his bed, happy that he had been able to get back into the happy routine of his life.

§

Fin awoke feeling someone watching him. He looked down at Ursula. In the darkness of her corner, he could just make out the shape of her little body, sound asleep.

He lifted his head and looked around his room. That's when he saw that the French doors to his balcony, under the clerestory window, were standing wide open. And he could see the shadow of someone standing there in the open doorway.

A series of quick thoughts flashed through his head. The first was that Suzy couldn't sleep and was looking out over the hills. Then, he remembered, with some chagrin, that Suzy wasn't here. His next thought was that someone had broken in to his house and was standing in his bedroom. That jarring realization was accompanied by the wish that he had a gun. He hated guns, but at a time like this, a pistol would certainly come in handy.

He reached for his lamp. Without a weapon, he didn't know if more light would help or hurt his chances, but he at least wanted to see who was there.

As soon as he switched the light on, he wished he hadn't.

The pale grey face drew no warmth from the lamplight. The skin looked thin, almost translucent, and was stretched tightly over the bones. But the creature's pallor wasn't, in itself, what sent a chill through Fin's body.

The eyes were dark, wholly black, the starkness of each orb intensified by the absence of any white around them.

Dark as obsidian, but without the visual relief of reflections. As lifeless as the shark's eyes that Captain Quint described in *Jaws*, no light shone on or from them.

Fin, his breaths coming fast and shallow, pushed himself up in bed, trying to get as far away as possible, but was hindered by the headboard and wall. As he moved, the creature's lips quivered and opened. That's when Fin saw the teeth. Not the short, softly-rounded cuspids from vampire costumes and movies, but inch-long, razor-sharp fangs, perfectly suited to piercing skin and veins.

In the few brief seconds that had passed, Fin, in the back of his mind, knew that there was no such thing as vampires. What he was seeing couldn't possibly be real. But a couple of years ago, he knew just as staunchly that ghosts weren't real, either. His time with Suzy had convinced him otherwise.

Whether it was a real vampire or not, Fin knew, or at least suspected, that ghosts could assume different shapes, and he knew from personal experience that an attack could produce physical effects. He desperately called to mind details of what they had done in the forest above Silver Plume more than nine months before.

"Go through the door, into the light," he said. He grimaced, completely unsatisfied with the tone and steadiness of his voice. He almost didn't blame the vampire for smiling at his timid suggestion.

He didn't have time to regret the quality of his command, however, as the vampire leapt upon him with astonishing swiftness, pushing him back down flat on the bed. Fin screamed as his hands gripped the cold, lifeless flesh of the creature. It felt almost dusty in his hands, the smell of mold strong in his nostrils. Attempting to keep its teeth away from his neck, Fin felt the nails of the vampire ripping his shoulders and chest.

With his left hand, he gripped the vampire's right arm, and in his acute panic, Fin was squeezing it as hard as he could. Unexpectedly, he felt the upper arm start flaking away, disintegrating in his grasp. The arm crumbled away below the shoulder, just as lifeless as before, but no longer moving, in Fin's hand.

Unfortunately, the sudden loss of an arm didn't deter the creature from its single-minded attack. Its now unencumbered shoulder slammed into Fin's chest, putting its mouth closer to Fin's neck.

Fin threw the musty arm aside and, screaming in desperation, tried to force the creature away from him. But every time he grasped it, the portion of the body that he grabbed disintegrated in his hand, yet it never stopped the creature. Fin, scrambling now in absolute terror, rocking back and forth on his mattress, was flinging dust in all directions as the teeth finally found their mark, piercing his neck.

Fin felt the sudden jab as the fangs ripped through his skin, and the wet heat of his blood pulsing out of his neck. He felt the cool lips of the creature set themselves against his skin, and he felt the suction as his blood flowed into the mouth of the vampire.

To his dismay, Fin felt his ability to fight flowing out of his body with his blood, his body relaxing in a lethargy unlike any he had ever felt before. Even as his body weakened, he could see the vampire's skin becoming more vibrant. The pallor was gradually being replaced by a pink glow, fed by Fin's own blood.

The texture of the creature, moisturized by Fin's juices, lost its dusty quality and became new and elastic. Pieces that had flaked away in Fin's hand healed. A new arm sprouted from the shoulder where it had come off, regenerating and becoming alive and strong.

The creature grew heavier on his chest, having drained Fin of his blood. He felt his heart struggling to pump as it was no longer able to draw liquid through his veins. His room was growing darker as his vision faded, and he knew that he was moments from death.

The vampire sat upright, now, its lips stained with Fin's blood, and it smiled at him. The yellow teeth were outlined with thin lines of blood trapped in the narrow spaces between them.

Suddenly, the creature leapt into the air and vanished in a cloud of dust, and Fin felt a rush of air down his throat as his diaphragm abruptly relaxed. He wondered how he was still conscious, though, and he managed to sit up. The French doors were closed. Still, the event was real enough that he was surprised at the absence of vampire dust on his covers. The dusty arm was not to be found on the floor where he threw it.

Ursula, though, was pressed as far back in her corner as she could get, looking at Fin in terror.

§

As Fin scrolled down the page on his computer in his library, he wasn't really surprised at the lack of results in his search for an animal exorcist. He could scarcely believe he was actually searching for one. But he knew it's what he needed. He had come to the realization when he thought about each individual episode.

He had killed a spider, after which he had the terrifying dream of the spider attack in the woods. Ursula was sleeping on the floor in front of the sofa.

When he was thinking of possible names for Ursula, he had mentioned Cujo. The spirit picked up on that and made it appear that Ursula was trying to rip him to shreds.

He remembered making a remark to the dog about her fiery-looking fur, and filling the house with warmth. That night he was driven out of his burning house into the snow.

Yesterday, after feeling a stab behind his eye from the bright light outside, he quickly closed the blinds. Once again embraced in the relative darkness, he had remarked to Ursula that he was becoming a vampire. The revenant obliged by becoming the terrifying blood-sucker that Fin had unsuccessfully battled hours before.

He was dealing with a contentious and combative spirit, and he wasn't strong or experienced enough to send it on its way by himself. He needed help.

The priest he called that morning wasn't helpful at all. He seemed to think it was all a big joke. Fin couldn't really blame him.

He sighed and looked down at Ursula. For now, she was sleeping peacefully in the bed that Fin got for his library. She seemed so calm. She could get excited, of course, but she didn't climb the walls or bark in ancient foreign tongues or vomit pea soup.

Maybe that was just demonic possession.

He had to admit, though, this ghost seemed pretty demonic, based on the hostile interactive visions it had forced him to participate in so far. If only he could make contact with it, and convince it to move on to the next plane or whatever they call that. Suzy was the expert, although she would say she's far from it. Still, he had never actually made contact with a ghost before, other than being threatened by one. This was his first time, the moment he had been dreading since Suzy insinuated that it could happen.

He sat back in his chair and rubbed his face. He couldn't get the image of that cadaverous, black-eyed vampire out of his head. That had been the most terrifying event of his life, despite the fact that it didn't actually happen.

If Fin couldn't find someone to handle this, he hated to think about the alternative. It was tempting to think of multiple alternatives, but there really was only one option that he could think of. He knew he couldn't take Ursula to an animal shelter where she could be adopted by someone else. That wouldn't be dealing with the problem, but only foisting it onto the next person. The only alternative he could see was euthanasia.

He looked at Ursula again. Fin had always had a soft spot for animals. He knew he couldn't do it himself. He would have to delegate it to someone else. And he would have to explain why he was having a perfectly healthy dog put down, and likely be thought of as crazy, or a monster.

He wasn't so sure he would be able to disagree with them.

And if it came to that, would the spirit even allow Ursula to be put down? If the ghost is this aggressive and violent when there was no provocation, what would it do when its host is threatened?

Fin sighed and turned back to his computer. He had to find an answer.

# 10

"'m beginning to think that maybe this wasn't such a good idea," Suzy grumbled.

"What are you talking about?" Rachel asked, looking around at the nearly-completed dining room.

"This decision to remodel my house. If anything, it's only making it worse."

"Your house?"

"Me!"

"Huh?"

Suzy sighed and turned around, walking into the living room, where Brian and Mike had just started working that day. The ghostly shapes of the furniture sat in the middle of the room, under their drop cloths. They had left a few minutes ago, and the smell of old plaster dust still hung in the air.

"All it's doing is stirring up the memories, not putting them away."

"I'm not sure I understand. You didn't really expect that the memories would go away, did you?" Rachel asked as she followed Suzy.

"Well, no, of course not. I know I'll have the memories for as long as I'm alive, or as long as I have my faculties."

"Exactly. The memories are in you, in your mind and heart, not in the house. These things you and Mark did here are just reminders."

"I know, and I feel like such an asshole for getting rid of them."

"No, you just don't need them anymore." Rachel's face brightened as a thought occurred to her. "Do you remember when you were in school, and you were assigned to memorize something from a book? You kept a bookmark there so you could turn to it and find it quickly while you were trying to remember it."

Suzy nodded.

"By the time you memorized it," Rachel continued, "you knew it so well that you not only remembered the part that you memorized, but you could picture where it was, which side of the page, how far down. You knew it so well that you didn't need the book to be able to quote it, but if you did need to find it, you knew exactly where to go. You didn't need the bookmark anymore."

Rachel gestured toward the stacks of old trim that had been taken down.

"This stuff is just a bookmark that you don't need anymore, because you remember. And now you can move on to your next assignment."

Suzy raised her eyebrows at Rachel.

"You're saying Fin is my next assignment?"

"In the realm of this particular analogy," Rachel smiled, "yes, he is."

Suzy returned the smile, but it was short-lived. She shook her head.

"I don't know. I had such a good thing with Mark and Emma. How can I have the audacity to expect that a second time?"

"Fin's not Mark. Don't expect the same thing. It's not audacious to want to find happiness, whatever form it might take."

Suzy looked at her friend with admiration.

"There you go, being all wise again," she said.

"I know," Rachel replied with a shrug. "It's what I do. My middle name is Gandalf."

"Did you just make a nerdy movie reference?" Suzy asked in surprised delight. "You usually just roll your eyes when I do that."

"For one's wisdom and experience to be accepted and applied, it must be expressed in language which the intended recipient can understand and relate to," Rachel replied glibly. "Either that, or else you've just been an incredibly bad influence on me."

"Well, if Fin doesn't give up on me and my lunacy, you may have two of us to contend with."

"I hope so," Rachel replied with a warm smile and a hug.

# 11

The hours scuffed by, dragging Fin along with them. He sat back in his chair, staring blankly at his computer. His search had, he felt, ultimately been unsuccessful. Out of desperation, he had taken a drive earlier, to buy some sage smudge sticks. He had burned them in his house, based on suggestions he had seen on a few web sites, but he wasn't very optimistic.

The day had slipped by with him accomplishing virtually nothing. No writing, no solution to the Ursula issue, and he was out of ideas. His tired eyes dropped down to the little dog again.

She had seemed jumpy all day. She would sleep for a few minutes, but if Fin moved at all, if the leather of his chair creaked, or if he tapped a little too hard on a computer key, she would jerk awake and look up at him.

Probably wondering what kind of craziness Fin was going to act out next.

"Poor little thing," he sighed. "I know you didn't ask for any of this." Once again, Ursula tilted her head as she listened to him. When he said nothing more, she put her head back down on the edge of the bed, but still looking up at him.

Fin wished he could get back to his story, but his head was too foggy. Besides, that last vision had just creeped him out too much. The Cujo attack was what inspired the story, and it was scary, but not entirely otherworldly. The fire, too, had been terrifying, but it was a fairly common fear.

Vampires, though, were something that he had never truly been afraid of. They were fodder for stories and movies, but not something that had ever seemed like a credible threat in real life.

Now, everything had changed.

He knew that the attack wasn't real, but that didn't matter. He had experienced such fear when he saw the creature, had felt the pain of his chest and arms being ripped by its claws, his neck being punctured by its fangs. He had felt his warm blood being sucked out of his neck by the vampire, and felt his body growing cold. To Fin, that was as real as it gets, and he hoped he would eventually be able to use those feelings in his writing. But for now, it was a little too fresh.

Ursula's eyes closed as she slipped back into sleep. Despite the fear that had settled over him, Fin could appreciate the inspiration for her name. Ursula K. Le Guin had been the one who had initially inspired him to start writing. When he read *A Wizard of Earthsea* as a boy, without the knowledge of his religious parents, of course, he was enthralled with the tale of the young wizard, Ged, and his mentor Ogion. Fin eagerly followed Ged's growth through his training at the school for wizards, and his confrontations with the dragon, and ultimately with the shadow creature that Ged himself had unwittingly released. The story had inspired him, not only to read the other books in the series, but to start composing his own stories.

He thought it was only fitting that he honor the author in this way. He only wished his relationship with the dog could be a little warmer, and a little less material for his ghost story.

He looked out the doorway of his office. The blinds on his window were still closed, but he could see the deep shadows in the hall. Feeling the fatigue weighing on him, he realized, with deepening distress, that he needed to go to bed again.

§

Fin awoke to a deafening sound, a deep, rumbling roar. He didn't even have to lift his head to see its source. The dragon loomed over him, filling his room, its back pressed against his cathedral ceiling. Its black wings were unable to open as they were bunched against the walls. The monster loomed over Fin, filling his room, yet somehow, moonlight found its way in to illuminate dull grey highlights on its scales. The great beast's head tilted down toward him, yellow smoke coiling up from its nostrils.

"Why did you summon me, little wizard?" the dragon asked. Its voice was deep and dry, its piercing green eyes watching Fin closely.

There was something vaguely familiar about this. Fin struggled to remember, as he sought to drive away the fearsome beast.

"I didn't summon you."

"You brought me here to your little cave," the dragon said, flames dancing above its three-forked tongue, "when I wished to stay on my island across the sea. Why have you disturbed me?"

Suddenly, something clicked, and Fin remembered.

"I did not bring you here, Yevaud."

The dragon jerked its head upward, surprised to hear its name spoken. Its great wings rattled, as if the dragon was preparing to fly away, but then, the dragon began to change. The wings pulled inward and disappeared into the body. The scales, once sharply outlined by the moonlight, became formless, the dragon's head and body abandoning their recognizable shape and becoming, instead, an amorphous darkness hovering over Fin's bed.

The shadow was deep and dark, absorbing any light that touched it and revealing no features. The edges of the thing pulsed and swirled, appendages appearing briefly, sometimes with sharp claws.

Fin watched petrified as the shadow hung poised over him. He knew what was about to happen, and he felt powerless to stop it.

The shadow drew inward, the darkness further intensifying to an unimaginable blackness. Fin felt it pulsing above him, sensed its anticipation.

Without warning, the thing fell upon Fin, ominously silent, its claw slashing and tearing, as Fin struggled to keep it at bay. Being a formless blob of darkness, though, it was impossible to hold it off. Each time he grasped the creature, it seemed as if his hand simply pushed through the shadow and he scrambled to find another handhold. Screaming and flailing his arms, he felt the razor-sharp talons tearing through his skin, saw his blood fly in dark crimson spray with each hack of the claws.

Finally, surrendering in exhausted agony, he lay still, knowing that death was seconds away. Then, just as suddenly as in the previous visions, the thing vanished, and Fin looked down at himself, his skin intact, his sheets free of any hint of blood splatter.

Panting for breath, he shook his head and pushed himself up on his elbow, looking down at the terrified little dog.

"Oh my god, Ursula," he said between gasps, "what are you doing to me?"

## 12

Pressing the phone to her ear, listening to Fin tell about his latest night terror, Suzy could tell that Fin wasn't himself. She could hear the fatigue in his voice, and she knew it was weighing heavily on him.

"Honey, I'm so sorry," she said. "That sounds so intense! I wish I knew what to tell you to do."

"I know. I'm out of ideas, too."

"Can you take a nap? I mean I know that doesn't address the main issue of the visions, but at least you wouldn't be so exhausted."

"I don't know. I tried a couple of days ago, and I was afraid to go to sleep. But by the time night falls, I'm so tired, I can't fight it anymore." Fin sighed. "If I could just make my mind blank and stop giving this damn ghost material to work with . . ."

"What do you mean?"

"Well, I realized that the visions were actually coming from my own suggestions. I toyed with naming Ursula Cujo that first day, and that night, I was attacked by a crazed dog. I mentioned her fiery fur and my house caught on fire. I said I was becoming a vampire because of avoiding the bright sunlight, and I was attacked by one that night. And yesterday, I was thinking about the book by Ursula K. Le Guin that got me started writing, and last night, I was attacked by the shadow monster from that story."

"Wait," Suzy said, "you said you were just thinking about that book?"

"Yeah," Fin replied hesitantly, wondering what Suzy's issue was.

"You're certain you didn't say anything out loud?"

"No, but I was thinking very clearly about it. I remembered reading the book and being so inspired by it that I started writing my own stories. They were pretty bad, to start with, but it's what got me on this path."

"But if you didn't say anything out loud, it couldn't be a ghost."

"Why not?"

"Because ghosts can't read your mind."

"Are you sure?" Fin asked, feeling his theory begin to crumble. "I thought they were capable of all kinds of supernatural powers. I mean, I know they can fly, they can move through walls . . ."

"They can do those things because they're no longer bound by a physical body in the physical world. But a ghost doesn't have the ability to read someone's thoughts any more than a living person does."

"Wait a minute, though," Fin said, trying to think coherently. "Aren't you reading their minds when you see their episodes?"

"It's not the same thing," Suzy said hesitantly. "I'm not really sure how to describe it. I'm only seeing what they're allowing me to see, what they're showing me, after I've made a connection with them. I'm not just picking their thoughts out of their minds, nor are they doing that with me. The visions are flowing through that psychic conduit that connects us. I know that all sounds very weird and New Agey, but that's kind of how it works."

"But," Fin stopped as if he were laboriously trying to piece his thoughts together, "if it's not a ghost, then why is this happening to me all of a sudden?"

Suzy paused for a moment.

"Well," she finally said, feeling a tightness developing in her chest, "I hate to bring this up, but have you considered going to a doctor?"

"You think I'm crazy?"

"No, I don't mean that kind of doctor." She paused again and took a deep breath. "Fin, you've been having a lot of headaches, and now these vivid hallucinations. What if it's something really serious, like a brain tumor, or something like that?"

A couple of silent seconds passed before she heard Fin's response.

"Shit," he whispered.

## 13

Fin had, surprisingly, been able to get in to see a doctor right away. Not *his* doctor, though.

"I'm sorry," the receptionist had said on the phone, "Dr. Randall is no longer practicing. His patients have been taken by other doctors in the clinic."

"I'm so surprised," Fin had said. "I had no idea that Dr. Randall was retiring."

"Well, he didn't retire," she replied hesitantly. After a pause, she continued. "I suppose there's no harm in telling you, since it's been in the news. Dr. Randall was arrested a week ago. He's been accused of several charges of medical malpractice." Fin hadn't watched the news, so this information was news to him. "Dr. Munroe has an opening this afternoon, if you're interested."

He was. After setting up the appointment, Fin had spent a couple of nervous hours looking up news stories online about Dr. Randall. Apparently, his doctor had been a little too generous with prescriptions, and a little too lax in explanations and follow-ups.

Now, sitting there in the examining room, he watched Dr. Munroe, a middle-aged man with a grey fringe around his otherwise bald head, as he studied Fin's record on his computer.

"I see here that Dr. Randall prescribed Mizaide nose spray for your migraines," Dr. Munroe said, still peering into the computer screen.

"That's right," Fin replied. Dr. Munroe looked at him.

"How has that been working for you?"

"Great! It works like a charm. The effect is almost instantaneous."

"How often do you use it?"

"It varies. A little more often recently. Extremely bright light seems to be the main trigger for me, and with the snow we've had in the last couple of weeks, alternating with the sunshine," Fin sighed, "I'm afraid it's been fertile ground for migraines. In fact, recently, I've been using a spray or two in the morning, for preventative maintenance. Why, is that a problem?" Dr. Munroe lifted one eyebrow and turned back to the computer.

"Did Dr. Randall go over the possible side-effects with you?" he asked evasively, typing a bit into Fin's record.

"Not that I recall."

"Did you read the warnings on the insert that came with the medication?"

"You mean the poster-sized sheet with small-type on both sides?" Fin replied a little sheepishly. "No, I don't think I did. Why?" Dr. Munroe raised both eyebrows and looked at Fin.

"One possible side-effect is hallucinations," he said. "It sounds to me like you may have fallen into the group of patients who have experienced them."

"Hallucinations?" Fin asked. He wasn't sure whether to be relieved it wasn't a brain tumor. "Why does it only happen at night? Why don't I have these hallucinations during the day?"

"Well, some studies have suggested that the active ingredient in Mizaide accumulates in the parahippocampal regions of the brain. This is one part of the brain that is instrumental in REM sleep. Some scientists have found that at night, when you relax and approach the dream state, that this is when Mizaide users are most susceptible to hallucinations."

Fin had visions of migraines dancing in his head as he considered the idea of going off the medication. Against his better judgment, he began weighing the possibility of cutting back on it, but not discontinuing it altogether. The drug worked so well at keeping his migraines at bay.

"Also, Mizaide is an opioid-based drug," Dr. Munroe continued, "in the same class as morphine and heroin, so dependency can be a very real danger. Dr. Randall really should have been keeping tabs on this." Dr. Munroe looked back at the computer.

"Shit," Fin thought. A newsreel ran through his head, memories of John Belushi, Philip Seymour Hoffman, River Phoenix, Heath Ledger, and others who died from opioid use, prescription or otherwise. He didn't know what he would do if he couldn't use Mizaide. He would have to re-sign himself to a life with migraines.

§

As Fin made his way back toward home, he stopped at a red light. It was not a busy intersection. Nobody else was there. They were probably at the malls, doing their Christmas shopping. Fin hated traffic signals that were timed rather than controlled by traffic, but he never went through them. It would be just his luck that a cop would be nearby and give him a ticket.

Sitting there, waiting, he thought about his visit with the doctor. Nothing was really resolved. Dr. Munroe had mentioned the Spotswood Institute, a local facility that was experiencing a fair amount of success in treating migraines and neurological disorders. Fin said he would consider it.

He kept his head down a little, allowing the brim of his hat and his dark glasses to shield his eyes from the bright sunlight flooding in through his windshield. He sighed, feeling warm and relaxed, but he became alert very quickly when a movement in his rear view mirror caught his eye.

Several police cars were bearing down on him, their lights flashing urgently. They were rushing toward him in both lanes, toward some unknown emergency ahead, and Fin knew he needed to get out of their way. The light was still red, so he decided to turn right.

As he did, though, he saw several more police cars and emergency vehicles coming toward him from that direction, filling the entire width of the street. In a panic, he veered to the left, not realizing that his car had jumped the curb. He jolted out of the hallucination when his car smashed through a short retaining wall and plummeted down a steep grassy hill, crashing into the asphalt of the access strip behind an industrial park.

He was unconscious when the *real* police and emergency vehicles arrived.

ello, is this Suzanne Quinn?"

"Yes, it is," Suzy replied, curious about the call from a Colorado area code.

"Ms. Quinn, this is Sherry Gilbert. I'm a nurse at Littleton Medical Center in Littleton, Colorado. I'm calling on behalf of Finley MacKinley. You're on file with his doctor as an emergency contact."

Suzy's heart jumped into her throat. She could hear her pulse pounding in her ears, and she felt a relapse of the fear and anguish she experienced over three years ago when she lost Mark and Emma.

"What's wrong?" she asked frantically. "What happened?"

"I'm afraid Mr. MacKinley was in a car accident. He's currently unconscious, but in stable condition."

"Oh my god!" Suzy exclaimed. "Is he going to be alright?"

"He has a fractured ulna," the nurse said, as if reading a list from his chart, "a fractured tibia, a concussion and several lacerations and contusions . . ."

"Okay, a broken arm, a broken leg, a concussion and cuts and bruises," Suzy interrupted impatiently. "And he's unconscious. *Is he going to be alright?*"

"Yes, ma'am," the nurse replied brusquely, "as I said, he's in stable condition. He'll be here for a couple of days, at least, for examination and tests, but eventually, he should be fine."

"Thank you," Suzy said, and she punched the disconnect button on her phone. Sinking down onto her sofa, she cried, partly from relief and partly from the momentary fear and anxiety.

§

On short notice, and this close to Christmas, the earliest flight she could get to Denver was the following evening.

That was okay. She had a few things to do between now and then.

The first thing she did was arrange for Rachel to be available, by phone at least, if Brian and Mike needed help or answers about any of the work, if Suzy wasn't available. Hearing the reason for Suzy's urgency, Rachel was only too happy to help.

She spent a couple of hours thinking about everything that she wanted Brian to do in the next couple of weeks, and writing out details, particularly finer points and variations from the plans that she had been considering. By the time she completed that, it was late, so she went to bed for a fitful night of sleep.

When Brian arrived the next morning, she told him that she had to leave town for an indeterminate amount of time, but she gave him an extra key, and Rachel's number if he needed anything.

As they worked, she went upstairs to start packing.

# 15

Fin opened his eyes and looked cautiously around him. He was lying in a hospital bed, his right leg and left arm partially immobilized. His head felt somewhat immobilized, too, and he realized he was wearing a neck brace. There was a faint but incessant beeping coming from the heart monitor beside the bed.

After a few moments, a pervasive pain started registering, which caused the beeping sound to speed up a little. With the pain came a hazy memory of what had caused it.

He looked toward the window. The blinds were down, but not quite closed all the way. He could see that it was dark outside.

The door opened and a red-headed nurse in blue scrubs breezed in. She smiled vaguely toward him as she focused on the equipment near the head of the bed. She did something that he couldn't see, and in just a few seconds, the pain eased a bit, and the beeps slowed down. Apparently satisfied, she looked at Fin again.

"How are you feeling, Finley?" she asked in a silky, calming voice.

What came out was something like a choked gurgling sound.

*Really smooth, Fin,* he thought to himself.

She smiled her vague smile again as she lightly patted his shoulder.

"It's been a few hours," she said. "Your throat's probably dry." She picked up a pitcher from his bedside table and poured some water into a plastic cup. As she held the straw to his mouth, he managed to suck a little down.

"Thank you," he said. "Call me Fin."

"Fin," Sara said. "Will do. You'll likely feel drowsy for a while. We have you on medication to help you manage the pain, and if you need anything else, just let me know. My name is Sara."

She looked around and noticed that the remote had fallen down at the side of the bed. She bent over and picked it up, and the V-neck of her scrubs hung down a bit, giving Fin a brief flash down her front. He quickly looked away. She moved the remote so that it was in easy reach.

"Thank you," Fin managed to say in a faint whisper. He was already feeling sleepy again, probably from the pain medication. He didn't notice when Sara left the room.

It was a couple of hours later when he woke up with a start. Again, the monitor reflected his alarm, but he didn't want to wait for a response to that. He felt the remote by his hand, and he pressed the button on it. A few seconds later, Sara came in.

"Hey, sleepyhead," she said with her smooth, calming voice, and that faint smile that Fin was beginning to recognize as her trademark. "How are you feeling?" He liked the fact that Sara didn't do the stereotypical *we* thing that nurses often did. "How are *we* feeling?" Finding that irritating, Fin immediately liked Sara a lot.

But he didn't have time to dwell on that.

"What time is it?" he asked.

Sara glanced at her watch.

"It's almost eight o'clock."

"Where's my phone?" Fin asked urgently.

"It's safe," Sara replied. "It's with your clothes and other possessions."

"I need to make a phone call!" He saw Sara start to try to calm him, but he barged ahead. "I have a dog. I need to arrange for my neighbor to take care of her."

"I see." Sara smiled and nodded. "Okay, don't worry. I'll see to it."

"Thank you," Fin sighed.

He stayed awake long enough to call Marian Anderson. She assured him that she still had the key and that Ursula would be cared for. She wished him a speedy recovery, and Fin disconnected.

Relieved of that worry, Fin drifted into a dreamless drug-assisted sleep.

§

Sometime in the morning, Fin opened his eyes and, in the dim light of his room, saw Sara doing something with the equipment beside his bed. When she saw that he had opened his eyes, she smiled that faint smile at him.

"Good morning, Fin," she said, and Fin marveled at how velvety and peaceful her voice sounded. "How are you feeling?"

"Better," he replied. "I really needed that sleep!"

"Good," Sara said. "You're looking better, too." Fin followed her eyes and saw that the covers were pulled down to the top of the cast on his leg. His hospital gown was pulled up, and there in the middle of it all were his genitals, in full view. And his dick wasn't just lying there innocently, but was pulsing, growing erect.

"Oh my god!" Fin exclaimed, reaching down with his right hand to cover himself, but Sara stopped him.

"It's okay, Fin," she said. "I'm a nurse. It's not like I've never seen that before."

She took his penis in her hand, and Fin felt it surge to fully hard and erect. She looked at him and her smile deepened. Then, as Fin panted for breath, Sara pulled her scrub top off, revealing the breasts that he only caught a brief glimpse of earlier. Sometime between then and now, she had removed her bra. She dropped the top on the floor, then pushed her pants down. As she stepped out of them and straightened back up, Fin was mesmerized by the way her erect nipples pointed upward.

Sara climbed up on the bed, straddling him, careful, he noticed, to avoid putting pressure on his leg. Fin saw a trim little patch of red hair, just in front of where Sara was guiding his penis.

She started moving up and down on her knees and moaning, obviously enjoying her impalement as much as

Fin was enjoying watching her breasts bounce up and down above him.

The only distraction was an insistent beeping beside his head. With the brace still around his neck, he laboriously turned and looked at the equipment and saw the numbers displayed there climbing as the beeps sounded faster.

He caught a movement in his peripheral vision and turned to see the door open. There was a brief moment of panic at being caught, before he saw Sara coming through the door, fully-clothed. As a wave of perplexity swept over him, he saw that he was covered, and alone, in bed.

He couldn't miss the rather prominent lump under the covers, though. He lifted his left knee in an attempt to look as if he were just innocently changing positions. He was sure Sara noticed, but she was giving her attention to the beeping equipment.

"We've reduced your pain medication a little," she said. "How are you feeling? Are you in pain?"

"No," he said quickly, and hoping he didn't look too guilty.

*Sorry Suzy. But at least I didn't almost die this time.*

# 16

"Hi, bud," came a familiar voice from the door. Fin felt a feeling of disorientation at the sound. He lifted his head and saw his parents as they filed into the room.

"Dad? Mom?" Fin's head throbbed and he laid it back down. He found the remote and raised the head of his bed a little. "What are you doing here?"

"You're our boy," his mother said. "You're having a bad time. Why *wouldn't* we be here?"

"Well, you haven't been for a while." The disorientation was persisting.

"The hospital called us," his dad said matter-of-factly. "They told us you were in a bad accident."

"Yeah. Apparently my Tesla's all but totaled."

"Was anybody else involved?"

"No, just me."

"Well, that's good. Nobody else was injured." His dad looked at Fin for a moment with an inscrutable expression. "Were you drinking?"

"Was I –" Fin made a scoffing sound as he looked at his father. "No, Dad, I hadn't been drinking. Why would you assume that?"

His father put his hands up as if fending off an unfair accusation.

"I didn't know." His voice was the voice of someone trying to reason with an unreasonable person. "It's just that you were in an accident that didn't involve anybody else. The roads are dry, nobody else around. And I know you like your Scotch." Fin exhaled again and turned his head toward the window, as much as the neck brace would allow. The blinds were closed, but they were glowing with bright morning sunlight. "I'm sorry. I didn't mean to assume."

Fin pondered for a moment. He decided that coming out with the truth and getting it over with would be the best course of action.

"I was having migraines, and the medication my doctor prescribed had some side-effects. It worked great, but it also has some dependency issues and, for me, caused hallucinations."

"Oh, honey," his mother said quietly, with a disappointed tone.

"So, are you saying that you're addicted to this drug now?" his father asked.

"I don't know, Dad," Fin replied, his voice taking on a rebellious tone. He felt like a disobedient teen again. "It's too soon to tell."

"Finley, we're just worried about you," his mother said. "We don't want to lose you."

"You're the ones who chucked me out. I didn't measure up to your rules, and you cut me off."

"They're not our rules, son," his father said, resuming his reasoning tone again, "they're God's."

"If God told you to jump off a bridge, would you do it?" Fin asked, smirking a little at the snarky turnabout of the question his parents had asked him on more than one occasion in his younger years. He felt bad about the expressions on their faces in response, but he couldn't help it. "Yeah, I suppose you would. You believe it was a perfectly legitimate request for God to tell Abraham to kill his own son. What's one more life, right?"

Fin saw the tears fall from his mother's eyes, and he turned back toward the window, feeling a little ashamed of his harsh and smartass response. Several seconds passed in silence.

"Have you heard anything from Kay?" his mother finally asked.

"No, Mom, not for quite a while now," Fin replied without turning from the window. "Couples don't tend to have a lot of contact after they get divorced."

"I was so sorry when you two got divorced. She was such a nice girl."

Fin smiled mirthlessly, remembering Kay's drunken naked dancing debacle at the Beltane festival a couple of years ago.

"It seems to me," his father said sadly, "that that was the beginning of the end. You divorced her, then you started getting famous for the dirty stories you were writing. Then, the last we heard, you were in an immoral relationship with some other woman and dabbling in spiritism."

"Oh my god," Fin said, turning back to them. "You really think that my getting out of a miserable marriage, and getting money and recognition for doing something I love are bad things?"

"If they're things that violate God's laws, then yes, son, I do."

"Un-fucking-believable," Fin said under his breath and turned back to the window.

"Finley!" his mother exclaimed.

"You've gone astray," his father continued, "but it's not too late. Do you remember Jesus' parable of the prodigal son? He squandered his money on booze and prostitutes. But when he came to his senses and turned his back on that ungodly lifestyle, his father welcomed him back with open arms."

"Can't you both just be happy for my happiness?" Fin asked, looking back and forth between the two of them.

His father made a point of looking at the casts on Fin's arm and leg, and looking around the hospital room.

"This makes you happy?" he asked.

"Oh my god, Dad," Fin said, losing his patience, "I'm talking about my life, not just my current situation. Yes, I'm very happy now, yesterday's accident notwithstanding."

"Okay, I get it," his father replied in a calming tone. "But if you draw away from God, he'll draw away from you. Look at you now." His voice quickly took on an exasperated, conceding tone. "Yes, I know your current condition is not your life, but you're all beaten up from a car accident.

You totaled your car while under the influence of drugs. You've been haunted by demons. These are just a few of the results of the decisions you've made. I'm afraid you're reaping what you've sown, bud."

Fin looked at him in disbelief.

"Your father's right, honey," his mother said, "it's not too late. You can still come back."

"Come back to an organization that encourages its people to disown and shun family members who don't toe the line? No thanks."

His mother pressed a soggy, well-used tissue to her eyes, then pulled another one from her purse. His father heaved a disappointed sigh and looked at his wife. He tilted his head toward the door.

"Well, we were hoping you'd see the error of your ways," his father said sadly, "that this would be a wake-up call for you. But we can't force you."

His mother uttered a sob as his father started guiding her toward the door.

"This may be the last time you ever see us," he said as he pulled the door open, "at least until you come to your senses." Fin's mother looked at him through her red, teary eyes. "We still love you, bud," his father said.

"It shows," Fin replied.

They turned and walked out, pulling the door closed on the sound of his mother crying.

"I love you, too," Fin said.

God, his head was throbbing!

§

"I've spoken with one of the two doctors who run the Spotswood Institute," Dr. Munroe said. "One of them, Dr. Ivanov, has actually worked with patients in the past who had addiction and dependency issues. So he'll be able to tailor your treatment with that in mind."

"Hmm," Fin replied, distracted.

"Is something wrong?"

"What? No, I'm sorry. I just never thought I'd be one of those people. Somebody who needs to get checked into rehab to get off drugs."

"Well," Dr. Munroe said, "Spotswood isn't a rehabilitation facility."

"No, I know," Fin replied quickly. "I guess I'm just feeling kind of sorry for myself." He tried to perk himself up. "So, when am I going?"

Dr. Munroe looked at his watch.

"Paperwork is complete. You'll be discharged from here and transferred to Spotswood in about an hour."

"Okay. Sounds good."

Fin tried to mold his face into an expression that looked like he actually meant it.

ust after 5:00 p.m., Suzy's plane started taxiing toward the runway at Logan International. The plane was full, and the large man sitting next to her forced her to lean a little toward the wall, inclining her head next to the window. She held Fin's latest book, *A Place Made of Time*, in her lap, but she had yet to open it.

Her head was a jumble of thoughts. They ranged from memories of Mark and Emma, and that fateful October day when she lost them just off the shore of Marblehead, to Fin and her deepening feelings for him, combined now with the thought that she had almost lost *him*.

She didn't know for sure what those thoughts were pointing to. She could disconnect herself from Fin, and from any future relationships, thereby protecting her heart from future pain. She remembered the Simon and Garfunkel lyrics, "If I never loved, I never would have cried."

In a way, that appealed to her on a certain level. To be insulated from the pain and sorrow that so often come because of unforeseen consequences of relationships with other people? How freeing that would be! Just think of all the pain she could have avoided if the last several years had never happened. And how much she could avoid by cutting it off with Fin.

She knew, though, that the line by Tennyson, "Tis better to have loved and lost, than never to have loved at all," was true. As much as she missed Mark and Emma, nothing could convince her to give up those few years she had with them. And the more she came to know Fin, the more she knew that she couldn't break it off.

Her plane stopped short of the runway, waiting in line for its turn to take off. She looked out the window at the grey sky and the gritty snow that blew around, settling in corners and crevices, sticking to anything that it was able to grip.

She couldn't get rid of the dread that was weighing on her. She had been so worried about Fin. His recurring headaches and hallucinations had to be something serious, and she couldn't stop thinking about the possibility of a malignant brain tumor.

Fin told her that he had an appointment with the doctor yesterday afternoon. Then, he had a serious car accident that put him in the hospital. Had he crashed on his way to the appointment, or was he upset with the news that he had learned and crashed afterwards? She wished now that, when the hospital had called, she had asked to speak to a doctor to get more information.

The engines revved and the plane inched forward and stopped again.

There were also regrets going through her mind. The old ones, of course, related to Mark and Emma. Why hadn't she just shut up about taking the boat out that last time when Mark made it clear that he didn't want to go? That was the main one.

But there were new regrets now, as well. She wished she hadn't been so focused on the renovation and redecorating of her house. She should have just done what she ended up doing anyway, leaving a key with Brian and Mike, and she should have gone out to Colorado to spend Christmas with Fin. Not that that would have prevented his hallucinations, but it might have prevented this accident.

Failing that, she should have, at least, dropped everything and went to Fin after the first hallucination. He was so terrified, and felt so unqualified to deal with a ghost on his own.

Of course, it turned out to not be a ghost, but at the time they didn't know that. And in the end, it turned out to, possibly, be something even more serious.

She should have been there to support him before now.

The plane moved forward again and turned. The engines rumbled and the plane surged forward, building up speed down the runway. Suzy watched the grey speed by out the window. One small portion of the composite roar quieted as the wheels lifted off the runway and the landing gear locked into place in the plane's belly, as the plane climbed into the sky.

Suzy sighed and opened the book.

# 18

The Spotswood Institute was named after Colonel Robert Spotswood, who was not actually a colonel. The title was honorary. Robert Spotswood had made a name for himself in the eighteen hundreds as 'wagon master of the high plains' and, later, as one of the owners of the Colorado Stage Company.

In time, Spotswood settled down southwest of Denver where he married Jessie Broad and they started a family. Though he was a devoted family man, he remained influential in the business and government of the neighboring towns of Wynetka and Littleton, Colorado.

The structure the Spotswood Institute occupied was built in 1900, an imposing brick building near the South Platte River, west of downtown Littleton, and not far from where the Spotswood family's home had been located.

Despite the antiquated exterior of the building, The Spotswood Institute had been fully restored inside to make it a state-of-the-art medical facility. Drs. Uri Ivanov and Judy Weinberg had personally supervised the renovation to insure it was up to their standards, and suitable for the work they would be doing there.

§

The flames were back, only this time, it wasn't his house that was burning. It was his room in the Spotswood Institute. There was an insistent beeping next to his head, but it was slowing, becoming erratic.

Fin turned and looked at the machine. The monitor that displayed his pulse, blood pressure and other arcane data to the doctors and nurses, was warping in the heat, the screen melting, the numbers blurring. It finally bubbled and the data stopped, as did the beeping.

Fin was surprised that heat intense enough to melt the hospital equipment wasn't doing damage to his own body. He could feel it, of course, but he wasn't burning up. He was just basking in the agonizing heat, the flames dancing all over his covers.

He was having a difficult time breathing amidst the inferno, and his mouth was hanging open, seeking a breath of fresh air.

"Are you still happy, bud?"

Fin turned to the other side of his bed. There was his dad standing in the flames. His mother was standing behind him, dabbing her eyes with a tissue.

As quickly as the hallucination had started, it was over. The flames were gone, the monitor was still beeping, quieter and less intrusively than it had in the hallucination. He felt chilled with the sudden disappearance of the flames, and he pulled the covers up.

At least it seemed that the hallucinations were getting shorter. But the image of his parents standing comfortably in the flames stayed with him.

§

"I don't understand," Fin said. "I've been taking Mizaide off and on for a few months. Why am I suddenly having hallucinations?"

Dr. Ivanov had come to meet Fin minutes after he had arrived at The Spotswood Institute. He took a position at the foot of Fin's bed as they talked. He was not a tall man, but his thick head of salt and pepper hair added a couple of inches.

"It happens differently, and at different times with different people," Dr. Ivanov replied with a heavy Russian accent, pushing his shock of hair back. "For some patients, it never becomes problem. But for others, drug takes time to accumulate to level that will make brain react and cause hallucinations."

Fin had told him that he had a couple more hallucinations that day. He kept a few of the details to himself.

"I haven't taken Mizaide in three or four days. Why am I still having hallucinations?"

"Have you heard of acid flashback, Feen?" Fin tried to nod. "Well, Mizaide is not LSD, of course, but it can work in similar ways, in that ingredients accumulate in brain, and effects show up later. Some patients have reported at least mild hallucinations as much as two years after they stop taking drug.

"According to your records," he glanced down and scanned Fin's record on the electronic tablet in his hand, "you have not used it for long time, so your symptoms may alleviate sooner, perhaps een week or less."

"Well, that's good," Fin replied, relieved.

"Yes, ees good," Dr. Ivanov agreed. "Bad news ees that if dependency develops, it does not take long. According to several studies on affected patients, by time hallucinations begin, patient has already developed some level of dependency on drug."

Fin's face reflected his disappointment and discouragement at this news.

"Do not worry, Feen," Dr. Ivanov said, his face breaking out in a wide smile, "you are een best place for this. We have much experience with this thing. We will take good care of you."

Fin sighed and nodded, trying to look as optimistic as Dr. Ivanov.

§

Fin lay in bed in his dimly-lit room in the Spotswood Institute. He had been sleeping, but had awoken a few minutes before. As he lay there in the dark, he was aware of various discomforts relating to the accident, as well as a strange sensation in his head.

As he lay there, an unusual sound caught his ears, the sound of a lot of people speaking indistinctly. Maybe it wasn't even speech. He couldn't be sure.

From his hospital bed, he looked around and saw rows and rows of people, little more than shadows in the gloomy area. The people were moaning, writhing in torment. They looked like the souls of the damned in illustrations of Dante's *Inferno*.

From among the mass of people cowering closest to his bed, a pretty woman rose from the squirming horde in front of him. She seemed oddly out of place. The expression on her oval face was sweet and demure, her abundant brown hair pulled up and arranged on her head in an old-fashioned style resembling that of a 'Gibson Girl.'

Unlike the Gibson Girl, she was naked.

With her head tilted downward slightly, she looked up at Fin with large, brown eyes. Her expression was indistinct, her mood indecipherable, but her gaze was intense.

She continued standing there in front of Fin, almost as if she welcomed his scrutiny. Her skin was soft and fair, like exquisite alabaster. Her body was curvy, with full breasts and a narrow waist.

She stood there looking at him, unaware or unconcerned about her lack of attire. As Fin was held spellbound in the woman's almost passionate gaze, he heard the sound of hoofbeats clacking on the hard tile floor, growing louder the nearer they came, as a large, dark brown horse stopped behind her.

The woman's lips curved slightly into a soft smile. Then, she turned and, somehow, climbed up onto the back of the glossy animal. She looked back at Fin one last time, then turned and rode away between the rows of the damned, her hair coming down and billowing behind her in her Godiva-like ride.

As she disappeared in the distance, details of the scene became obscured in darkness and clouds, the writhing masses swirling like a dark van Gogh painting, until it all went black.

As Fin watched, he saw his dimly-lit hospital room reappear around him, as a nurse came in quietly to check the monitors by his bed. Instinctively, Fin raised his left knee as he had the last time.

"Are you in pain?" the nurse asked. His arm and his leg were sore, and his head throbbed a little, but he was already spooked about drugs now.

"No," he said quietly, "I'm fine."

ncluding a short stop in Chicago, just long enough for a quick dinner at the airport, Suzy's flight lasted five hours. By the time she got her rental car and drove to the hotel in southwest Denver, it was almost ten o'clock local time. According to Suzy's internal clock, it was nearly midnight.

She didn't take the time to unpack anything but her toothbrush. She fell into bed and slept through the night.

In the hotel's restaurant the next morning, she ate a quick breakfast. While she waited for her food to arrive, she took out her cell phone and called the Littleton Medical Center.

"Could you put me through to Fin MacKinley's room, please?" she asked.

"One moment, please," the receptionist said. There was a long pause, during which Suzy heard the sounds of a general hubbub in the background. Must be a busy morning. "I'm sorry, ma'am," the receptionist said when she finally came back on the line, "we have nobody by that name admitted here."

"But a nurse called me the day before yesterday and said that he had been in an accident and had been admitted. Has he already been released?"

"He must have been." The woman sounded uninterested, or distracted.

"Thank you," Suzy said and disconnected.

She tried Fin's number. Pressing the phone to her ear, it never rang at all, but went straight to voice mail. She frowned, wondering what was going on.

One thing that kept intruding into her brain was the thought that he had died. She knew it was unlikely. It was a ridiculous thought, but after Mark and Emma, she couldn't help it. Logically, she knew the injuries that the nurse mentioned on the phone a couple of days ago didn't sound that serious. Even the nurse herself said that, in time, he should be fine.

Still, unexpected complications happen all the time. She remembered hearing about a famous actress a decade ago receiving a relatively minor bump on the head while taking a beginner's skiing lesson. Two days later, she died of an epidural hematoma, as a result of that bump.

Fin was in a car accident and received a concussion from, most likely, much more than a minor bump on the head. So while dying from his injuries wasn't out of the question, by any means, it was a thought that she had to repeatedly and consciously reject.

§

After a fruitless forty minute drive to Fin's house, with the help of the GPS app in her phone, Suzy was still mystified, and no closer to figuring out where Fin was. Feeling even more nervous and concerned, now, she drove to the hospital, determined to get some answers.

She was glad she had gotten an early start. It was almost ten o'clock by the time she got to the hospital. Two days after the fact, she decided to go to the main desk instead of the emergency room.

"Good morning," said a thirty-something woman with faintly pinkish-blonde hair. Her name tag said Roxanne. "How can I help you?"

"I was told a couple of days ago," Suzy explained, trying not to sound as upset as she felt, "that my friend was brought here after a car accident. I got here as quickly as I could from Massachusetts, but I was told this morning that he's not here."

"Oh, I'm sorry," Roxanne said. She seemed genuinely concerned, and Suzy liked her immediately. "What's your friend's name?"

"Fin MacKinley."

"Let's have a look," Roxanne said as she tapped in the name and perused her computer screen. After a few seconds, she smiled. "Finley MacKinley? That's cute."

"Yes, that's him!" Suzy said, relieved.

"He *was* here," Roxanne said, "but he was transferred to a different facility last night, The Spotswood Institute." She reached for a piece of scratch paper and wrote down an address. "I'm sorry about the confusion this morning," she said as she handed it to Suzy. "We were inundated overnight with a multi-car accident on C-470, and some of our departments got a little behind in updating records."

"Thank you so much!" Suzy sighed.

"Of course," Roxanne smiled as Suzy turned and ran out the door. Once she made it back to her rental car and got inside, the relief washed over her in an overwhelming wave, and she cried.

§

After the tears of relief stopped, Suzy realized that she didn't know what The Spotswood Institute was all about. Was Fin transferred there because his injuries were more severe than the hospital originally realized, and they determined he needed specialized treatment? Or worse?

She remembered a scene from an old movie from the 70s, *Coma*, in which brain-dead coma patients were kept artificially alive in the stark and cold Jefferson Institute, waiting for black-market buyers for their organs.

With a frustrated sigh, she pushed that thought from her mind. She pulled up the GPS app on her phone and typed the address for The Spotswood Institute. It was only five minutes away.

The dark brick building, very different from the more modern homes and buildings nearby, brought back the ominous feelings she had experienced earlier, but she knew she was just being silly and irrational. Walking inside, she was greeted by a bright reception area which, while modern, still managed to celebrate the turn-of-the-century styling of the exterior. The young man at the reception counter was dressed sharply in a business suit, very different from the hospital environment.

"Good morning," he said. "What can I do for you?"

"I was told that Fin MacKinley was admitted here last night," she said.

"And you are?"

"Suzy Quinn." She hesitated slightly. "His fiancée."

Fin had hinted a couple of times about marriage, but he had had the good sense to not push her about it. However, in the current situation, Suzy thought that his fiancée might have a better chance of being able to visit him than his long-distance girlfriend.

"If you'd like to have a seat," the young man said, motioning toward a seating area, "I'll check with Dr. Ivanov and see if Mr. MacKinley's undergoing any treatments at the moment."

"Thank you," Suzy replied before turning and sitting down in a comfortable armchair. The young man picked up his phone and spoke briefly, and quietly, with someone, before putting the receiver down.

"Dr. Ivanov will be out in a moment," he said. Suzy nodded her thanks, but wondered again what kind of facility this was. It was obviously not a typical hospital.

After a minute or so, a frosted glass door opened near her, and a fiftyish man with greying hair emerged.

"Ms. Queenn?" he said with a smile.

"Yes," Suzy said, rising to her feet and shaking his outstretched hand.

"I am Dr. Ivanov," he said with a heavy Russian accent. "I am een charge of Feen's treatment. How can I help you?"

"I was hoping I might be able to see him. I just arrived late last night from Massachusetts, but I don't know when your visiting hours are."

"We do not have strictly-enforced visiting hours. If patient ees agreeable and not een middle of treatment, visiting ees fine." He pulled the door open. "Come with me."

Suzy followed him through the door into a gleaming white hallway lined with what looked like examining rooms and labs. A computer tablet was mounted outside the door of each examining room. They were removable, Suzy noticed, as a doctor took one down and consulted it before entering the room and greeting the unseen patient, closing the door behind him.

Dr. Ivanov stopped and pressed a button at the elevator.

"What kind of facility is this, Dr. Ivanov?" Suzy asked as the elevator rose.

"We do eenpatient and outpatient treatment of neurological issues. Een Feen's case, we will be starting regimen to treat his migraine headaches."

"Oh, so his being here has nothing to do with the car accident he was in?"

"No, no, his injuries are serious, but not that severe. We are fully equipped medical facility, so we will continue monitoring injuries, of course, but his migraine issue ees reason why he ees here."

The elevator stopped at the third floor and the doors opened.

"This ees floor for eenpatient rooms," Dr. Ivanov said as he led the way down a somewhat less institutional-looking hallway than the one on the first floor.

"It looks like a very nice place," Suzy said.

"Yes, we try to make patients comfortable during their treatment. And toward that end," he motioned toward Suzy, "we encourage family to visit, when tests or treatments are not underway, of course."

"Of course," Suzy replied. "And I don't want to be in the way."

"Nonsense. We have not begun Feen's treatment, yet. We are still studying his records and results of blood tests and X-rays we've taken. We'll allow day or two for him to heal and settle before we start treatment." He stopped outside a door. "This ees Feen's room. Very nice to meet you, Ms. Queenn."

"Thank you, Dr. Ivanov." Suzy smiled at him and pushed the door open.

Suzy was a little shocked to see Fin, his left arm and right leg in casts. There was a collar around his neck, and a bandage taped to the left side of his forehead. A large portion of the left side of his face and head was a greyish-purple color. He seemed bored as he watched a large TV mounted on the wall. Suzy's entrance captured his attention, sparking his interest much more than whatever was on TV.

"Suzy!" he exclaimed, turning the TV off. "What are you doing here?"

"Well, you'll apparently do anything for sympathy. So, against my better judgment, I just came to give you the attention that you're so desperate for." Having had her fears assuaged by Roxanne and Dr. Ivanov, she had to admit that it felt good to embrace her snark again.

Fin smiled.

"What an incredibly pleasant surprise." He seemed to speak cautiously, careful to not move much. "This seems too good to be true, so I'm thinking it must be a hallucination. Although, given the last couple of ones I've experienced, if this was a hallucination, you'd be naked."

"Intriguing," Suzy said, taking his right hand in hers. "Maybe later. I *would* like to come back to those last two hallucinations –"

"I'd rather not."

" – but for now," she glanced at his casts, "what's going on with you?"

Fin's expression dimmed.

"I'm a drug addict."

Suzy gave a confused frown, and Fin explained what had happened in the last couple of days, starting with his appointment with his replacement doctor and learning about his dependence on Mizaide, and the hallucinations it produces.

"So no brain tumor!" Suzy said, feeling her relief become complete.

"Thankfully, no."

"Oh, honey," Suzy sighed, "I'm glad. I've been so worried about you."

"I'm sorry I didn't call you," Fin said contritely. "It didn't occur to me that the hospital would notify you about the accident. I guess I should have thought of it, after my folks showed up."

"You saw your parents?" Knowing his history, Suzy was as surprised as Fin had been.

"They came to the hospital yesterday morning. They let me know that God's rejected me, and they reconfirmed that they have too."

"They didn't really, did they?"

"They said it would be the last time I would ever see them, unless I come to my senses and come crawling back as a prodigal son."

"Assholes!" She shook her head, then she looked up at Fin. "Sorry, I know they're your family, but people who could treat their own son like that are beyond my compassion. It makes me angry that they could treat someone I love so badly."

"Thank you," Fin said with a grateful smile.

"How are you feeling about it?"

"I wish I could say that I just let it roll off my back. Obviously I'm sad and pissed. And I'm afraid there's also a bit of guilt."

"Guilt? Why?"

"Well, I've turned my back on the way I was raised. All my life, practically everything we did was with God in mind. If we weren't sure about something, we'd ask, 'would God be displeased with me if I did this?'"

"I guess it must be hard to break away from a faith you've had all your life."

"I don't think I ever really had the faith," Fin replied thoughtfully.

"But you were raised with that mindset, hoping to not displease God."

"That's just it. It was a mindset, for me, at least. It was never in my heart. Just an underlying fear of eternal punishment if I disobeyed God's laws."

"So you *did* have faith."

"I had fear. I'm not sure that's the same thing."

"Hmm," Suzy pondered.

"Anyway, I've left that mindset. But it's still there, sometimes, in the back of my mind."

Fin made a scoffing sound.

"Interestingly, it wasn't until later that the feeling of guilt set in. Since my transfer here wasn't an emergency, they didn't have the siren going in the ambulance. Instead, they were playing Christmas music. *God Rest Ye Merry Gentlemen* came on, and the third line hit me over the head."

"To save us all from Satan's power when we were gone astray," Suzy recited. Fin nodded.

"Dad used that very word, that I had gone astray."

Suzy sat on the edge of the bed and leaned forward, embracing Fin, her head resting on his chest. Fin was warmed instantly by her love and sympathy. He hugged her back with his right arm.

"I can't tell you how wonderful it is to see you!" Fin said. "I've missed you so much."

"I've missed you, too," Suzy confirmed, planting a kiss on his lips. "I'm sorry I didn't come sooner, when you started having problems."

"I am too, but I understand. I'm not the only thing going on in your life."

"That's true, but you *are* the most important one." Fin sighed and held her tighter. "By the way," Suzy added, "I just thought I should let you know. It looks like we're engaged now."

# 20

ood news," Suzy said. "You're not a drug addict." She had pulled a comfortable armchair, similar to the ones in the lobby, close to Fin's bed and spent the day there while they alternately talked, browsed notifications on their phones and did research.

"How do you figure?" Fin asked.

"Says here that there's a difference between dependency and addiction," Suzy replied, reading from her phone. "With dependency, you build up a certain tolerance for a drug, and you might have a physical need for it in treating pain or whatever it was prescribed for. Due to that tolerance, you may need to take more of it in order to receive the same relief.

"Addiction, though, is more of a psychological thing. You *crave* the drug, even after it's no longer needed for a physical treatment. You need it, not for relief from pain, but for the high the drug itself provides. While dependence has the intention of improving the condition of the individual, addiction is the contrary, where the individual only reaches a higher level of self-harm."

"Hmm. Maybe I won't go to hell after all."

"Well, you do still write those dirty books."

"True," Fin conceded with a nod. They both smiled, taking comfort in the humor of an otherwise painful situation.

Suzy put her phone down and looked at Fin.

"So you think that last hallucination was suggested by your parents' visit?"

"That's my guess. Part of it, anyway. The damned writhing in agony in Dante's hell is probably what I have to look forward to. Not that I really believe in hell. No idea where the naked Gibson Girl and the horse come in, though."

"That's what you called her when you were relating the dream to me, but I didn't want to interrupt, and then I forgot by the time you were finished. What's a Gibson Girl?"

"That's a term that came about at the turn of the twentieth century, based on pen and ink drawings by a popular illustrator of the time named Charles Dana Gibson. His portrayal of women of that time were so popular that they were known as the Gibson Girl, and became a fashion ideal for women. They had certain physical characteristics, like attractive faces and curvy, hourglass figures, long hair piled casually but neatly on top of their heads, and they always wore nice, fashionable clothing.

"But there were other features, too, features that both men and women liked. A combination of beauty and intelligence, fragility and strength, voluptuousness and grace.

"The woman in my hallucination, despite her lack of the fashionable clothing, seemed to display all of those qualities."

"Hmm. Maybe you were just missing me," Suzy suggested with a grin.

"Ha!" Fin scoffed. "You thought I missed you?" His expression softened, unable to maintain the taunt for very long. "Only every hour of every day."

§

At five o'clock, an orderly brought Fin's dinner and left it on the rolling table by his bed.

"I should go," Suzy said. She was touched by the disappointed look on Fin's face.

"Aw, really?" he said.

"I need to get some dinner for myself," she said, "and get some rest, and let *you* get some rest, too. I've taken up your whole day."

"That's right, thanks to you, I've missed my daytime TV viewing regimen for today. I don't think I can ever forgive you for that."

Suzy smiled as she picked up her purse and put her phone away. She looked at Fin and got serious for a moment.

"I'm so glad you're okay," she said.

"Yeah, aside from being destined for hell."

"Oh, I doubt it'll be that bad. You'll be in pretty good company anyway. Based on what I've heard from a few people, I'll likely be there myself."

Once the joke settled and passed, they held each other's gaze for a few moments. Finally, Suzy got up and sat on the edge of the bed.

"I love you, Fin," she said. He couldn't help but sigh as he looked at her.

"I love you, too, Suzy."

Suzy leaned forward for a long, comfortable embrace.

§

Walking in downtown Denver, he saw the Brown Palace hotel looming ahead of him. Built of sandstone and red granite, the three-sided Italian Renaissance Revival hotel stood tall on its triangular block between Broadway, 17th Street and Tremont Place. At nine stories and 143 feet tall, the architectural gem captured the attention of every visitor to the area.

The façade soared upward the closer he got. But suddenly, his attention was drawn to something else. He heard hoofbeats in the distance. As he turned and looked around, the sound grew louder until it was a thunderous cacophony filling his ears. To his horror, he saw the horses galloping directly toward him, northward up Broadway.

He threw up his arms in front of him and screamed as the heaving mass of dark brown horseflesh was upon him like lightning. He felt countless hooves pounding his body, crushing him into the ground. He could feel his bones breaking, his body turning to mush.

The horses continued on their way, oblivious of him, and he felt himself oozing into the dirt, seeping deeper into the ground. He had no idea how long it took, but it seemed like hours that the darkness enveloped him.

Finally, as if oozing feet or miles through the ground, he fell into whatever space it was that existed below the ground. He didn't have to wait long to discover what that space was.

The smell of sulfur assaulted his senses and the flames engulfed what was left of his body. The pain was unbearable. He tried to scream, but his head, like his body, was little more than a puddle of jelly, and he couldn't move. He couldn't open his mouth, if he even had one anymore.

All he could do was lie there in agony.

Eventually, the scene faded away. Panting for breath, he looked around at the shadows of his room in The Spotswood Institute. He never expected that he would be so happy to find himself a patient in a medical facility.

# 21

Dr. Judy Weinberg, Dr. Ivanov's partner, was in Fin's room. She was nearly six feet tall, with a prominent nose and dark brown hair, and she gestured profusely as she talked. She had dropped in to let Fin know that his migraine treatment would likely begin in the next day or so.

"It'll be a bit of trial and error to begin with," she said with a slightly nasal New York accent, "but our guesses will be educated ones."

She turned around when the door opened and Suzy walked in.

"Oh," Suzy said, stopping just inside the door, "should I come back?"

"No, not at all," Dr. Weinberg gestured with an exaggerated wave of her hand. "Come on in. You must be Fin's fiancée. I'm Dr. Weinberg." She held out her hand and Suzy shook it.

"Suzy Quinn."

"Pleased to meet you. I was just letting Fin know that we'll be starting in on his migraines in a couple of days."

"Wonderful! What will the treatment consist of?"

"It varies. We tailor the treatment specifically to each individual, based on a number of factors, including medical histories, blood tests, X-rays and so on. But it's usually a combination of pharmaceuticals and physical therapy."

"That's great," Suzy said as she went to the bed and stood beside Fin. Dr. Weinberg was pivoting constantly, to look at both of them as she talked, and it made Suzy nervous. "This must be costing a pretty penny."

"Well, due to Fin's injuries, the hospital was going to be keeping him for a couple more days anyway. He just traded his time there for here. Not counting the specialized treatments we administer, the per diem charges are comparable. And, of course, his insurance covers the majority of it." She shrugged and smiled, and waved her hand in a dismissing gesture. "Anyway, I'll get out of here and let you two visit. It was nice meeting you, Suzy."

"Thank you. You too."

After Dr. Weinberg left, Suzy turned and smiled at Fin.

"How exciting! I sure hope it works."

"Thanks," Fin said wearily. "I do, too."

"Whoa, bad night? You look really tired."

"Yeah, another hallucination. It was a bad one. I couldn't get back to sleep after it."

"Aw, honey, I'm sorry. I see they took the neck brace off." Suzy placed her hand gently on his neck. It was rough from a couple of days' growth of whiskers. "How does it feel?"

"It's sore, but it's nice to have a little movement back." His eyes were half-closed.

"You look like you're about to drift off," Suzy commented.

"The pain was worse this morning, and Dr. Weinberg upped my pain medication. So, besides the short night, the sleep is making me druggy." Suzy smiled, not knowing if the wordplay was intentional or not.

"Well, I won't think you're a bad host if you go to sleep while I'm here." Suzy settled in her chair beside his bed. "I'll just be a quiet little bookworm. As it is, you'll still be entertaining me." She held up *A Place Made of Time*. Fin smiled sleepily and was gone.

§

A slight movement tickled his leg, and he looked down. He just saw his covers draped over the contours of his legs, and rising up to go over the humps of his feet at the foot of the bed.

Probably just the otherwise imperceptible movement of a hair triggering a nerve ending. Happened all the time.

He closed his eyes again, feeling sleep drift over him. But there was that feeling again, this time on his other leg.

Fin lifted the covers and looked under them, but it was dark. He couldn't see anything. But he could feel it, more and more. There was something there. The sensation was building. Something was definitely moving against his legs. He pushed the covers off and was horrified to see both of his legs engulfed in writhing, squirming worms.

He might have been enthralled by the sheer variety, from the lowly maggot to large, brilliantly-colored horned caterpillars, slimy earthworms to ribbon-like tapeworms, if they had not been consuming his legs. But they wrapped around his limbs, turning them into bubbling lengths of slime, as they worked their way upward.

Fin, panting in a panic, didn't know whether to try to push them off of him or not. Somewhere in the back of his memory was the spider attack, and how his attempts to brush them off of him resulted in spreading them to his hands and, ultimately, the rest of his body.

Despite the terror of the situation, Fin felt no pain. But he could clearly see the mass of worms slowly collapsing as his legs disappeared into the frothy goo, and as their fodder dissolved, they made a concerted effort to move upward.

They advanced up to his pelvis and his belly, and in his anxious distress, Fin tried to push them off. His memory of the spiders, though, and the premonition that accompanied it, proved true, as some of the worms and the slime clung to his hands, working their way up his arms.

As tears engulfed his eyes, he frantically shook his hands, trying to dislodge the worms. He screamed when he felt one particularly large and forceful creature grasp onto his upper arm. In a frenzy, he tried to dislodge it, but it held fast. He grabbed it around its throat and tugged against its hold.

"Fin!" it said. Fin stopped, momentarily confused. "Fin, it's okay!"

He looked at the giant worm and saw that it was attached to Suzy, her hand holding on tightly to his arm. He followed it upwards, and he saw Suzy's face, her eyes wide with fright and concern.

"Honey, you're okay," she said, more softly now.

He looked at her for a moment, the terror giving way to exhaustion. He looked down at his legs, free now of the former larval feeding frenzy, and he let his head fall back on his pillow, and he dropped into welcome sleep.

## 22

Suzy didn't get much reading done. She spent most of the time that Fin was asleep watching him, alert to any signs of another hallucination, but he slept soundly.

She had no idea what he thought he was seeing, but it must have been terrifying. She was still haunted by the horror in his eyes.

After a couple of hours, he stirred, and Suzy was up, standing at his bedside, her hand resting softly on his arm. He opened his eyes and groggily looked up at her, and he smiled. Then, his breathing quickened as the memory returned, and an expression appeared on his face that could have been a combination of fear and embarrassment.

"How are you feeling?" Suzy asked quietly.

"I'm not sure," he replied shakily. "I think I had another hallucination."

"Yes," Suzy nodded, "you did. But you're okay now." Fin grasped her hand, holding on tightly as if it were a talisman. "What was it?" Suzy asked quietly.

Fin looked up at her and, besides the fear and embarrassment, he looked a little nauseated.

"I was being eaten up by worms," he said, barely above a whisper. Then, a look of recognition. "You mentioned being a quiet little bookworm."

"Oh my god," Suzy said, "that's all it took?" Fin nodded.

"It doesn't seem to take much. My brain snags a word or thought and dreams up some delightful experience for me to savor."

"Oh, honey," Suzy said, "I knew they sounded bad when you told me about them, but I was thinking they were more like nightmares. But seeing that look of terror on your face earlier, I can see now that I had no idea of the ordeal you were actually going through. I'm so sorry to have triggered it."

He shook his head but seemed too tired to respond.

"You're still sleepy, aren't you?" Suzy asked.

Fin nodded. Suzy smiled sympathetically and caressed his arm, and he slipped away again.

§

He was surprised when he woke up and found Suzy lying in his arms. But he wasn't disappointed.

He looked at her and kissed her forehead. At the touch of his lips, Suzy lifted her head and looked at him. She smiled, and she moved toward him for a long, passionate kiss, engaging their lips and their tongues.

When they finally broke away, he looked at her. But she wasn't Suzy. It was the Gibson Girl again. Somehow, she felt familiar, but he couldn't place her. Her hair, no longer arranged on top of her head, was draped across her shoulders and the pillow.

He felt her body, naked and warm against him, and he pulled her closer, caressing her soft curves. She smiled at him, but as he looked at her, her face changed again. It darkened, turning red, and horns pushed their way through her abundant hair. Her body turned hard and scaly, and when she kissed him again, he felt two points of her tongue probing against his.

She smiled and put her hands on him, and as he watched her face in engrossed fascination, he felt her pull him downward, through the bed, into some kind of dark void. He hovered briefly in the void, until she pulled him down further.

The darkness of the void gradually changed, the black turning to shades of red and gold, as flames licked at his body, blistering his skin. He tried to take a breath, but the heat and the pain were stifling and he couldn't get his body to work, trapping his breath in a limbo between inhalation and exhalation.

He looked at her face, and given the pain he was feeling, he was surprised to see that she was smiling. But she continued smiling as she pushed him down, apparently delighted by his agony.

As his skin charred and fell off of his bones in paper-thin flakes, he finally found his breath, and he screamed, writhing in misery. She laughed, evidently pleased with his torment.

Just before his anguish pushed him into unconsciousness, the flames disappeared. So did the Gibson Girl/devil hybrid.

§

As Fin gasped for breath, his room in The Spotswood Institute rematerialized around him, and he saw Suzy sitting in her chair. But she wasn't relaxing, or reading her book.

She was looking at Fin, gripping the arms of her chair, her eyes wide, as she gasped for breath.

What the hell was that?" Suzy asked.

"Wait," Fin replied, struggling to understand, "I don't get it. You saw it, too?"

"I saw it," she panted, "I felt it. Fin, that was no hallucination."

"What else could it have been?"

"That was a ghost. It had to be!"

"Hold on," Fin said, his face wearing a weary frown, "you said it *couldn't* have been a ghost."

Suzy, trying to get that experience out of her head, closed her eyes, attempting to focus her thoughts.

"The hallucinations you had at home, and a couple of hours ago, were just hallucinations," she said, "and Ursula is just a dog." She looked up at Fin. "But now, through some weird coincidence, or cosmic joke, you've ended up in a place that actually does have a ghost. And you've made contact. Or, rather, the ghost has made contact with you."

"A hospital with a ghost?"

"It's a hospital now. I don't know what it was before. But despite the sleek, ultra-modern interior, this is an old building. And there's a very restless spirit here. My best guess is that you're developing what my advisor, Lilith, calls your SpiritSense. You're able to pick up the visions that ghosts are willing to share with you."

"Shit." Fin put his head back, more exhausted than ever. "I never wanted that."

"I know, honey. I didn't either."

"So, what do we do?"

"Well," Suzy said, pondering, "this ghost hasn't exactly introduced himself. This crazy vision he's shown us so far hasn't really told us anything about him."

"Except for his fixation on hellfire and Gibson Girls," Fin replied. "And horses."

Suzy fished her phone out of her purse and woke it up.

"We need to start a dialog with this ghost, and then help him move on."

"You have his number?" Fin asked, watching Suzy use her phone.

"No, smartass," she replied with a grin, "but the first thing I'm going to do is find out about this place."

§

"Things they don't tell you when you check in," Suzy said when Fin opened his eyes. He had dozed a bit and Suzy let him sleep while she did her research.

"What?" Fin asked groggily, elevating the head of his bed.

"The structure was built in 1900 to house the Arapahoe County Asylum for the Mentally Ill," she read from her phone. "The conditions that prevailed were essentially the same as in many other facilities of its kind at the time. Overcrowding was common, with little thought to actual treatment of mental illnesses. To be fair, modern psychiatry was in its infancy, and social alienation and general mistreatment were to be expected."

Suzy scanned the article, looking for other information pertinent to their current curiosity.

"The asylum closed in 1942 after multiple charges of cruelty were leveled at several members of the staff. With the economy gearing more toward America's entry into World War II, it seems that the institution decided to settle with its accusers rather than embark on lengthy and expensive legal battles."

More scanning.

"A couple of other entities occupied the building in 1946 and 1957-58, but in both cases, they vacated quickly with little or no explanation. The building stood vacant for decades, in the face of several instances of pressure and threats of demolition. Each threat, though, was met with bitter opposition from those intent on preserving the historical architecture.

"During the economic recovery after 2008, incentives were offered to potential buyers. In 2014, the building was finally purchased by Drs. Uri Ivanov and Judy Weinberg to house their burgeoning neurological practice. The structure was gutted, followed by an extended overhaul of the interior. Due to several unforeseen problems, including equipment malfunctions and issues with contractors and other workers, the renovation exceeded both its budget and its deadline.

"In a nod to local history, Ivanov and Weinberg named their practice The Spotswood Institute, after Colonel Robert Spotswood, one of the settlers of Littleton. It finally opened for business in October of 2019."

"Wow," Fin said, "I didn't realize their practice was only a couple of months old."

"Out of everything I read," Suzy replied, "that's what you're taking from this?"

"Gimme a break, I'm frazzled."

"Sorry," Suzy smiled. "This building was an insane asylum, with charges of mistreatment of patients. And I'm sure it's safe to say that people died here.

"Then, after it closed down, it remained unoccupied for nearly eighty years, with only two tenants during that time, both of which didn't last long and left quickly. When the doctors finally purchased it and began the renovation, there were lots of problems, including equipment malfunctions and unnamed problems with the workers."

"Shit," Fin said, as realization settled on his face. "Sane ghosts weren't scary enough?"

§

Suzy closed her eyes and relaxed in her chair. She breathed slowly and steadily, focusing her mind on making contact, while Fin watched drowsily from his bed.

When she had actually engaged in two-way communication with spirits in the past, for the most part, it had been inadvertently, and just before drifting off to sleep. Suzy hoped she would be able to intentionally duplicate those results here.

She felt stirrings, flutterings of a presence, and she tried to fix her attention on it, to draw it in, but it was difficult. She didn't feel the same level of attention from the spirit. The impression she got was that it was unpredictable and mercurial.

As her relaxation waned and she became more tense, she was surprised to find the connection growing stronger. In the darkness of her closed eyes, she began to see something taking shape, though the shape was nebulous. A young, handsome man appeared, but he quickly changed to a grotesque figure covered in sores. That figure, in turn, changed to a figure whose skin was partially flayed from his body, to one whose flesh was burnt and blistered.

"What's your name?" Suzy asked, directing her thoughts to the spirit.

The shifting figures stabilized briefly on one that resembled a male form of Fin's Gibson Girl devil. The figure blurred, as if threatening to shift again. Finally, the handsome man reappeared and stayed, though his appearance flickered. He looked at Suzy with a puzzled look on his face.

"I'm Cole," he said, but it appeared to require some effort on his part.

"Cole, I'm pleased to meet you. I'm Suzy."

Cole seemed nervous, constantly looking around, glancing over his shoulder.

"It's alright," Suzy said. "You're safe."

"No," he replied. The fear on his face was palpable. "I'm not safe. I'm accursed."

"You're safe with us," Suzy emphasized, speaking calmly and soothingly. "We won't judge you. We're friends."

Cole seemed to relax a bit. His rapid breathing slowed. Suzy had become accustomed to such vestiges of life appearing in ghosts, things like breathing, crying, and so on, things that were familiar and that expressed humanity and feelings. She found that they were calming to her as well, helping her to accept them as extant individuals.

"Tell me about yourself, Cole," Suzy invited softly, her voice calm and velvety. She knew that people usually liked to talk about themselves. Cole looked at her, his appearance still flickering like multiple images superimposed on each other, different ones briefly gaining dominance.

In time, though, the handsome young man remained, and he became a bit more composed as his eyes sparkled with tears.

rthur Coleman, Cole to friends and family, gripping his one suitcase, was the first to step off the train and enter Denver's enormous Union Depot. It was early, and the sun had not quite come up yet. Few people were up yet, either, so there weren't many to get in his way as he walked through the station.

The darkness made the three story bronze-plated arch in front of the depot even more striking. Over a thousand electric light bulbs spelled the word, "Welcome" across the top of the arch high above his head. He smiled and nodded a mental thanks toward the greeting.

Right in front of the station, he was able to catch an electric streetcar heading south, the first one of the day. He shook his head in amazement at the modern conveniences of the big city. It was so different from the life he had left in the rural area outside of Centralia, Illinois. Still, what he was heading towards was probably closer to what he was accustomed to.

In a couple of days, he would be taking on his new position in the house staff of a ranch south of Denver. Although he thought the term 'ranch' didn't really do it justice. He had heard that the ranch sprawled over twelve thousand acres of prairie land south of the city.

By the time he reached the end of the streetcar line, a magenta sun had risen in the east, casting a gorgeous pink glow over the houses around him, and the mountains to the west. As he bounded down off of the streetcar, he saw, parked at the side of Broadway, facing south, a wagon hitched to a couple of horses. He smiled as he saw the driver looking over his shoulder.

"Good morning, Uncle Rupert," he waved, tossing his suitcase in the back of the wagon next to a box of supplies.

"Good to see you, boy," Rupert said. "How was the trip?"

"It was fine," he enthused as he climbed up on the seat next to his uncle. "This is quite a country."

"That it is," his uncle replied, slapping the reins against the flanks of the horses. As they started forward, Cole sighed and looked around again, especially toward the mountains in the west.

"It's great to be out here," he said. "I sure do appreciate you putting in a good word for me at the ranch."

"I was happy to do it, son. I just hope this situation turns out better for you."

"I do, too. I'm afraid Pop's not too happy with me."

"Yeah, I know how he can be. I grew up with him."

"Honestly, I think he arranged this just to get me out of his hair."

"Well, the Reverend's not exactly one to welcome embarrassment. Still," Rupert paused, thinking. He glanced at Cole. "I hope this high country air is good for you. That sort of thing won't be approved of at the ranch, either."

"No, of course not." Cole was quiet and pensive for a while, watching the outskirts of town slip by. "First time it happened," he finally said, "Pop thought I was blotto. But he finally believed me when I insisted I hadn't had anything to drink.

"He wanted to keep it quiet, but people still ended up hearing about it. I don't know for sure, but I'm guessing one of my brothers let it slip. Anyway, once people started asking about it, Pop tried to explain that I was receiving visions from God, but in time, the visions became anything but godly.

"The last one, though, was the final straw. It happened in church, when Pop was giving the sermon."

Rupert clicked his tongue and shook his head.

"What was it like for you?"

Cole looked at him briefly.

"Nobody's ever asked me that." He thought for a moment. "Sometimes it was like I was watching somebody else's life. I'd see things happening to them as if I was looking through their eyes. Other times, though, I'd see really strange things, scary things. Sometimes," he glanced at Rupert, and the rosy glow of sunrise hid the flush on his face, "shocking things. Things that," he hesitated, "things I don't want to talk about."

Rupert nodded and quietly watched the road.

§

It was nearly nine o'clock in the morning. The sun was climbing higher, as was the June heat, as they approached the house. It was much grander than Cole had expected. A large sign spanning the road proudly advertised:

Springer's
Cross Country Ranch

"This is a ranch house?" Cole asked in disbelief. "It looks more like a castle."

"It's funny you should say that," Rupert replied. "The master, John Springer, has named it Castle Isabel."

"Isabel?"

"His wife. Pretty young thing. About twenty-eight, thirty years old. A few years older than you. Springer's fifty. His first wife died of consumption a few years back. He married Isabel just three years ago, in 1907."

Cole watched wide-eyed as the stone mansion loomed larger the closer they got. Rupert drove the wagon around to the back.

"Wait here," he instructed as he climbed down off the wagon. "I'll be right back."

He hoisted the box of supplies out of the back of the wagon and carried them up the steps to the back door, toward the kitchen, Cole assumed. A couple of minutes later, he was back.

"You'll stay with me in the bunkhouse for the next couple of days," he said as the wagon started forward again. "I'll use what free time I have to coach you in your duties as footman."

"You know about such things, Uncle Rupert?"

Rupert cast a gruff glance at Cole.

"I started out as a footman years ago. Worked my way up to butler. Not here, mind you. Here, they don't stand on as much tradition and formality as some of the hoity-toity places I worked in back east, but they still expect a job to be done well.

"In times past, a footman's duties included going wherever the master and his family went, helping the women down from the carriage and so on. Nowadays, your duties are pretty much confined to the house. Besides your assigned duties, you'll also substitute for Mr. Gordon, the butler, if he happens to be indisposed."

Cole nodded, surprised at this revelation about his uncle.

*"Why aren't you working on the house staff now?"*
*Rupert looked at him again.*
*"I decided I liked horses better than people."*

§

*In his temporary berth in the bunkhouse that night, Cole lay on his bed, his Bible illuminated by lantern light. The passage he read, as it usually did, while giving him a sensation of excitement, also caused a feeling of guilt.*

> *This thy stature is like to a palm tree, and thy breasts to clusters of grapes.*
>
> *I said, I will go up to the palm tree, I will take hold of the boughs thereof: now also thy breasts shall be as clusters of the vine, and the smell of thy nose like apples. . . .*
>
> *Come, my beloved, let us go forth into the field; let us lodge in the villages.*
>
> *Let us get up early to the vineyards; let us see if the vine flourish, whether the tender grape appear, and the pomegranates bud forth: there will I give thee my loves.*

*Also, as it usually did, it made him remember Laura. The same age as Cole, she had been a good friend who, for one reason or another, was often thrown into his company.*

*Cole didn't mind.*

*She was pretty, her body having developed ahead of other friends her age, and she seemed to be cheerfully aware of the effect it often had on Cole. One time, a couple of years ago, she happened to be visiting, and Cole had asked her to pick corn with him. To his delight, she had agreed. It was late summer, and quite warm and humid, and by the time they had filled the basket with ripe ears, Cole suggested that they sit on the shady side of the shed to cool off.*

*Laura fascinated Cole. Her dark eyes and hair, he thought, were gorgeous, but her freckles seemed to cast a sense of innocence over her exotic beauty.*

119

But Cole also sensed a bit of danger in her that belied that innocence. Her family was not as strict as his was, and even within the context of her family, Laura seemed like something of a black sheep. He didn't know where she got that quality, but he liked it.

Cole was insanely attracted to Laura, and he thought that she felt similarly about him. There had been numerous times when she seemed to seek him out, whether after church or at church social events, or times like now, when she showed up at his house. The fact that she wore dungarees appealed to him, oddly enough. She wore dresses to church, and Cole thought she was beautiful in them, but wearing trousers just seemed rebellious, dangerous. For some reason, Cole found that exciting.

Back behind the shed, Cole couldn't remember what they had talked about before, but during the course of their conversation, their daily Bible reading program came up. Cole had just read The Song of Solomon, and it was quite fresh in his mind.

"I just wish we had some grapes and pomegranates," Cole said. Their conversations of late had flirted with their budding sexuality, but they had always been afraid to go too far. God was always paying attention.

"Grapes and pomegranates?" Laura asked, scrunching up her face in a questioning expression.

"Thy stature is like to a palm tree," he quoted, having read the verses over and over, "and thy breasts to clusters of grapes."

Subconsciously, Laura pushed her chest out a little, and she smiled at him.

"Well, that explains the grapes. But why pomegranates?"

"Let us get up early to the vineyards; let us see if the vine flourish, whether the tender grape appear, and the pomegranates bud forth: there will I give thee my loves."

Laura smiled and, squirming a little against the back wall of the shed, she turned a bit more toward Cole.

"You want my pomegranates, do you?"

He glanced at her chest, then quickly back at her face, but she had seen his distraction. It had been her intention, after all.

"I love pomegranates!" Cole replied, tingling with the naughtiness of the insinuation.

*Laura cast a quick glance around the corner of the shed toward Cole's house, then turned back to him. She started unbuttoning her checked cotton shirt as Cole watched wide-eyed. The stirrings he had felt in his groin as he quoted* The Song of Solomon *to Laura suddenly experienced a growth spurt as she opened her shirt, revealing her breasts encased in her brassiere.*

*The brassiere was little more than a layer of cloth, and Cole noticed how tightly the cloth was filled with her breasts, her nipples forming noticeable points in the otherwise virginal white fabric. He was thrilled to see the freckles on her chest, disappearing mysteriously behind the fabric.*

*He sat there frozen, looking at her bosom, and when he didn't make a move, Laura moved closer to him. She pulled her shirt off, then reached behind her and began unfastening the hooks of the brassiere.*

*When she pulled the brassiere off, he saw her breasts, the first breasts he had ever actually seen in real life, and he could barely catch his breath. Cole realized that his cocky attitude of a couple of minutes before, safely ensconced in the innocence of Bible verses, had now melted away.*

*Laura reached out and took his hand, pressing it against her breast. Holding it in his hand, Cole marveled at its softness, and at the contrasting hardness of her nipple.*

*"Oh, sweet Jesus!" he breathed. Laura smiled, moving closer to him, and she leaned forward. She placed her hand on his thigh, just inches from his privy member, to support herself as she kissed him softly on the lips.*

*The moment was shattered by a familiar voice.*

*"Cole," his mother called from the house, "do you have the corn?"*

*Cole stiffened up suddenly, as Laura pulled away laughing, snatching up her brassiere and shirt.*

*"Yes," he called, "I'll be right there!"*

*Cole watched Laura walk around the far side of the shed, toward the big, overgrown buttonbush, in case his mother came out to see what was taking so long. He was mesmerized by the graceful bobbing of Laura's breasts as she walked.*

From that afternoon on, he knew that those arousing verses in the Bible would never be the same again.

In his bunk, now, he kicked himself for opening to The Song of Solomon. He should have known better. He would have to ask for God's forgiveness for the impure thoughts he had allowed.

He directed his mind to other thoughts. He felt a pang of home-sickness, and he thought about his family. He had never been close to his younger brothers, Jonathan and Kenneth. Even as young boys, they seemed to sense that something was a little off with Cole. Cole himself recognized that, too, though he never liked to admit it. But he was always more attracted to cerebral pursuits than were his overly active and mischievous brothers. Most of his time spent with them was as the butt of one of their jokes.

His father, the Reverend as he was usually referred to, even by his family, was a cold and strict man. If someone crossed him, he considered that one lost to the devil, at least until he apologized and took steps to correct his course. Only then would the Reverend consider allowing that one back into his good graces.

With Cole, it seemed as if he recognized that flesh and blood required more forbearance. He didn't write Cole off right away. He allowed him a second chance, even a third, but it was a strain. The Reverend's face was stern and hard even when granting that mercy, as if it was quite a strenuous activity he was involved in.

Cole's mother was the one he had always been closest to. A meek and mild little woman, she always provided warmth and safety to her family, but especially to Cole, as if she knew that he needed her protection the most.

He remembered one noteworthy day when he was a little boy. It was a particularly hot summer and he had accompanied his mother as she tended the garden. They hadn't been out there very long when Cole was startled by the hollow clatter of a timber rat-tlesnake that was sunning itself near the woodpile that leaned against the shed a few feet in front of him.

Cole couldn't remember if he even understood the significance of that sound, but there was no mistaking the actions of his mother. She was instantly in front of Cole, placing herself between him and the snake. Grasping the hoe that was in her hands, she swung it upwards with all the determination and godly fortitude of Moses, as he prepared to split the Red Sea. She swung it downwards with equal force, cleanly chopping off the head of the snake. Cole was fascinated as the body continued writhing for a few minutes after being severed from its head.

When she was certain that the snake was no longer a threat, his mother dropped the hoe and turned around to Cole, engulfing him in her arms. His loving protector, soft and tender, yet courageous and strong, that's how he always thought of his mother.

It gave him a twinge of sadness that she hadn't felt well enough to see him off when he left home. She was the one he missed most of all.

## 25

Oh my god, that was so cool!" Fin raved as the room coalesced around him again. For now, his drowsiness had passed, but the episode, as Suzy referred to them, had left other feelings in its wake. He laid his head back, dizzy and exhausted, but clearly enamored by the experience. He put his hand up to his head as he took deep breaths.

"The dizziness will pass," Suzy said. "You'll get accustomed to it in time. At least the dizziness from the episode will pass. I don't know what kind of effect Laura's breasts had on you."

"So, you saw it, too?" Fin asked, choosing to ignore her remark about Laura's breasts.

"I did," Suzy smiled. "Once I was able to calm him down a little, we seemed to finally start getting a coherent story from him."

His excitement overcoming his exhaustion, and the fear he used to feel about Suzy's 'creepy' episodes, Fin sat up in bed.

"Did you catch his explanation of what his hallucinations were like?"

Suzy nodded.

"Sounds like he may have had a bit of SpiritSense himself," she replied. "Going into trances and seeing the lives of ghosts must have been especially tough for a preacher's son."

"Yeah." Fin was quiet for a few moments as he identified with Cole.

"I wonder if there were other issues with him besides seeing ghosts," Suzy contemplated, "or if that was the extent of his insanity, which got him placed here."

"The 'hallucinations' I saw after I checked in here looked pretty crazy. Burning in hell wasn't about just seeing someone else's life."

"You're right," Suzy shuddered, remembering the one she had seen.

"God, that's so weird."

"What is?"

"Well," Fin pondered, "insanity is a disorder of the brain, right? Or sometimes a physiological chemical imbalance or something like that."

"Right."

"Ghosts don't have brains," he continued, "or physical bodies. So how can insanity persist beyond death? How can his mental disorders still be presenting themselves after he's dead?"

"Hmm." Suzy took a breath and thought for a few moments. "I remember you asked something similar in Silver Plume back in April. Since then, I've done a little research on it, which ultimately yielded nothing. But I have some thoughts.

"Aside from genetic characteristics and physical attributes, almost everything we do, everything we are, the way we act, the way we think, to some extent, it all involves conditioning. Even treatment of mental disorders requires *re*conditioning, establishing new habits. Maybe that conditioning, those habits are things that transcend the body and brain."

"Sure. Maybe that's why some hauntings I've heard about involve ghosts repeating certain actions over and over."

"Could be. You know, besides their conditioning, I've seen other characteristics of physical, living beings presented by ghosts, too. Things that are familiar expressions of their living selves. Things like tears, or sighing."

"Or Caden's ghost still using a crutch."

"Exactly."

"Makes sense." As the faintness settled on him again, Fin laid his head back. It didn't stay there for long. He looked at Suzy with a different concern etched on his face. "So there's a ghost in this hospital. Do you think we should tell Dr. Ivanov and Dr. Weinberg about Cole?"

Suzy looked back at him, her eyebrows raised in a questioning expression of doubt.

"Do you really want your neurologists to know that you're seeing visions of dead people?"

Fin sighed, feeling even more fatigued.

## 26

The Springers were away for the first week of Cole's new position, so his duties were light. When they both had the time, Rupert continued coaching him concerning what would be expected of him in his position. Gordon, the butler, also provided some guidance, though Cole thought he seemed somewhat resentful of the need for it.

The house was indeed grand, although the interior seemed a little more rustic than he had expected, particularly the main living area. It was also a bit smaller than it seemed from outside.

For the first week, Cole was not plagued by his hallucinations, so he was encouraged that this move had been a good choice. At times, though, if he felt stressed, he found a place to go, a place that helped to calm him if his schedule allowed him time to make use of it. Less than eight hundred yards directly south of the house stood a windmill, recently built, the main structure of which was constructed of stone. It was a beautiful thing and, standing isolated on the prairie, Cole found it to be a peaceful place.

Sitting on the ground with his back against the stone tower of the windmill, Cole would gaze at the Rocky Mountains to the west, wondering at the wildness of such a wondrous place. Other times, he would look to the east, wondering how his family was getting on without him.

§

"You're new here," Isabel Springer said. Uncle Rupert had been right. She was indeed lovely. She smiled at him familiarly which made Cole feel uncomfortable, but in an exciting way.

The house staff had lined up to greet the Springers when they arrived, but they had now dispersed. However, Mrs. Springer had caught his eye and came to him.

Cole had seen a photograph of her in the house in which she appeared demure and refined, even shy. He was surprised at how genial and gregarious she seemed in person.

"Yes ma'am," he replied. "I'm the new footman."

"What's your name?"

"Arthur Coleman, ma'am."

"Arthur Coleman," she said, rolling the name around her mouth in a way that made him wish his name had more syllables. He squirmed a little, but tried to hide it. "Do people call you Artie?"

"No ma'am," he replied, feeling perspiration pop out on his forehead, "people actually call me Cole."

"Cole," she repeated, and she smiled again. "I like that. You can call me Sassy."

"Oh, no ma'am," Cole replied quickly. "I couldn't possibly!"

She glanced over at John, who was still directing Gordon about some detail of house business.

"Well," she whispered, "maybe just when my husband's not around."

She extended a finger and touched his shoulder, sliding it down his upper arm as she walked away, but she glanced back at him over her shoulder. She joined her husband, but she walked around to the other side of him, so she could look past him and see Cole.

Cole felt his knees going weak, and he knew he needed to get away before she said another seductive word to him.

§

A warm breeze was blowing from the west as Cole stood facing the mountains, the windmill cranking rapidly above him.

"There you are." Startled, Cole turned to see his uncle. He hadn't heard his approach.

"Oh, Uncle Rupert," Cole sighed. "I just needed to get out of the house for a few minutes."

"Something wrong?" Rupert asked. His eyes were squinted a bit, as if expecting bad news. "You're not having one of your visions, are you?"

"No," Cole shook his head, "nothing like that. I just met the Springers." He looked up at Rupert, disturbed. Rupert looked back at him, waiting for a more in-depth explanation. The next words Cole said, he whispered. "Mrs. Springer is on the make."

"What are you saying, boy?"

"She told me to call her Sassy," Cole said quietly but with an urgent tone. "She stroked her finger down my arm as she walked away. I truly believe she means something improper."

128

"You know you can't call her Sassy," Rupert cautioned.

"I know! I told her that. She said, 'just when my husband's not around.' Fortunately, Mr. Springer wasn't close enough to hear her."

Rupert looked at Cole, his head turned a little as he looked at him askance, not sure whether to believe him or not. Cole noticed the familiar expression.

"I'm not making this up, Uncle Rupert!"

"I didn't say anything, son," Rupert countered.

"I know. But I've seen that expression before. Pop used to make it a lot, when I started seeing things."

"It just seems to me that this is a dangerous thing to be seeing."

"But I'm not just seeing this," Cole insisted. "I'm not making it up!"

"Alright, alright," Rupert said, waving both hands in what he hoped was a calming gesture, "don't get yourself worked up. Mrs. Springer is a very attractive woman. I've not, personally, had any close dealings with her, but I admit I may have had an improper thought or two myself." He saw Cole's irritable expression, and he tried to calm him again. "I'm not saying you're imagining it, but maybe you're building a little on whatever she said or did."

Cole sighed and looked toward the mountains again. The breeze on his face helped to calm him a little. But not entirely.

"Those improper thoughts you had," he said, "how did you get rid of them?"

"I don't know that I ever did. They came back up right now when I mentioned them. The point is I never did anything about them."

"But Jesus said that 'whoever looks on a woman to lust after her has committed adultery with her already in his heart.' How do I get those thoughts out of my mind?"

"Sorry, son, but you're asking the wrong person. Your old man's the preacher, not me." Disappointed, Cole nodded and looked back toward the mountains. Rupert clapped Cole on the shoulder. "You'd best not stay out here too long."

Cole sighed and nodded again as Rupert turned and walked away.

*Looking toward the mountains again, Cole closed his eyes and felt the warm breeze wash over his face. It was calming – a little – but it didn't solve his problem.*

*He opened his eyes again, and he saw the mountains in front of him erupt in flames. The fire climbed up the peaks, sending black smoke into the sky, blotting out the sun.*

*As the mountains were obliterated, the fire quickly spread downward over the foothills, and across the prairie toward him, consuming everything in its path. Cole leaned his back against the stone tower of the windmill, holding his breath as he waited for the inevitable.*

# 27

Fin and Suzy came out of the episode in unison and looked at each other, both breathing heavily from the stress of what they had just witnessed.

"That was her," Fin panted.

"That was who?"

Fin took a deep breath and exhaled it.

"The Gibson Girl. It was Isabel Springer."

"You're right," Suzy said breathlessly as she recalled the episode. "I guess it's safe to say that the mountains weren't really wiped out in 1910."

"No, I'm pretty sure the ones out there now are more than just a century old."

"So he was having hallucinations, too. Not just seeing spirit episodes." Suzy shook her head sympathetically. "That poor guy. He apparently had some kind of affliction like schizophrenia, then, before he came out here, he may have channeled ghosts, and to top it off, he's plagued with religion-fueled guilt about it." She looked at Fin. "Reminds me of someone."

"Yeah," Fin nodded. "Can I just enumerate what I've been through in the last few days? I started experiencing terrifying hallucinations," he said, ticking the points off on his fingers, "that we thought must be the product of the visitation of a ghost or a malevolent spirit. Eventually, you determined that it wasn't that, but the terrifying hallucinations were actually coming from my own head. So, on my way home from finding out that I'm dependent on the drug that causes the hallucinations, I'm in an accident and wind up here, in a place that actually *does* have a ghost, who has seen visions of ghosts and has terrifying hallucinations, and is afflicted with religious-based guilt. What the hell are the chances?"

"There are some," Suzy said, "who claim that there are no coincidences. Whether you believe in God or fate or the universe as a living entity, things that we perceive as coincidences could be manipulated or orchestrated for the best outcome. Or the worst, depending on how much of an asshole the universe is."

"Well, if you'll pardon my negativity, it feels to me like the universe is shitting all over me."

"I know," Suzy said, reaching for his hand. As she took it, Fin squeezed it almost desperately, and Suzy realized how deeply the events of the last few days were affecting him.

§

"I'm here to start your migrainectomy," said Peter, the physician's assistant who breezed into Fin's room that afternoon.

"Hmm," Fin replied, "do you have to make it sound painful?"

"Oh, it won't be painful at all," Peter replied with lavish gestures. "You don't need migraines, right? We're just going to cut them right out of your life. The best news is won't cost you an arm and a leg, and you won't even need anesthetic."

"So, my concussion, bruises and broken bones won't interfere with this?"

"The bruises and fractures, no, not at all. And, based on the results of the tests we ran earlier, you seem to have come through the concussion just fine. So, Mr. MacKinley, it looks like you're a prime candidate for our award-winning migraine therapy."

Fin and Suzy both smiled at the good news, delivered in Peter just-below-the-surface flamboyance.

"Should I leave?" Suzy asked.

"You know," Peter said, looking at his watch, "normally I'd say you can stick around, but this will probably take us till dinner time. So it might be best for you if you go and have some dinner yourself, get some rest, and you can come back tomorrow."

"No problem," Suzy replied. She gathered up her phone, her book and her purse, then leaned over and kissed Fin.

Though Fin was sorry to see Suzy go, he was happy to get underway and, hopefully, put an end to his migraines.

oney," Rachel said, "it's probably best that you're not here. You'd probably freak out about the condition of your bedroom."

"Why?" Suzy asked apprehensively, relaxing in her hotel room as she spoke to Rachel on her phone. "What's wrong with my bedroom?"

"Nothing's wrong. Everything's going according to plan. But your bedroom is a mess. I just figured that, while you're in Colorado, this is the perfect time to move Brian and Mike in there."

"Really? I didn't talk about that with Brian before I left. I mean I did, but it's been a while."

"Don't worry. The plans are here. He knows what to do."

"You're right. Good idea." Suzy relaxed. She had already filled Rachel in on what was going on with Fin, and that the situation wasn't as dire as she had originally feared.

"You know, that Brian is kind of cute," Rachel added in a tone that sounded straight out of junior high school.

"Yes, he is," Suzy chuckled. "Have you asked him out yet?"

"Me? No." There was a pause. "I *have* put myself in his line of sight a few times, though. I'm pleased to report that it seems as if he has noticed me."

"Good," Suzy smiled. "I so appreciate you being there for me."

"I'll *always* be there for you. At least until Brian sweeps me off my feet and takes me away to some remote tropical island to indulge my every fantasy."

"I love you, Rachel," Suzy smiled.

"I love you, too, Suzy," Rachel replied. "Get some rest."

After they disconnected, Suzy couldn't help wondering what her bedroom must look like. She resolutely shook her head, deciding not to think about it. The thoughts that followed, though, she couldn't stop.

Mark had often referred to their bedroom as the boudoir, the haven or the rumpus room, depending on his mood at the time.

Or their activities.

Suzy remembered the first time she and Mark entered the bedroom after their wedding. They had come back to the house to change and get their luggage before heading off to Italy for their honeymoon.

As Suzy approached the bedroom door, Mark grabbed her hand and stopped her. He bent over a little and swept her up in his arms. Suzy gasped in surprise, but when she realized what he was doing, she recovered quickly.

"You know," she said, raising an eyebrow at him, "I have given evidence on numerous occasions that I'm actually able to walk on my own."

"I know," Mark replied with what sounded like an unimpressed tone, "you're very talented. Could you hold your skirt so I don't trip on it?" Suzy reached down and pulled the skirt of her wedding gown up out of the way and draped it over Mark's shoulder. "And could you get the door knob?"

"Jeez, do I have to do everything?"

Mark rolled his eyes in response as Suzy turned the knob and pushed the door open. He turned and carried Suzy across the threshold, into the bedroom. As he put her down upon her feet, Suzy turned and grinned at him, letting her smartass persona slip away.

"We did it!" she said.

"We sure did." Mark smiled back at her and placed his hands on her cheeks, leaning forward and kissing her gently. As he pulled away, Suzy gazed into his eyes for a few moments. Then, suddenly, she threw her arms around his neck and kissed him hard, hungrily.

"Damn, girl!" Mark said after she let go. He glanced at his watch. "You know, we don't have to be at the airport for a couple of hours."

Suzy smiled at him and was already pushing his jacket back off his shoulders. He allowed the jacket to fall to the floor as if oblivious to her efforts, and she started untying his tie.

"I think we should make some babies in this room," he said as he looked around at the bedroom they had recently decorated together. Suzy stopped and looked at him for a moment. Mark looked back at her. "Maybe not tonight, though. I want you all to myself for a while."

Suzy smiled as she ripped the tie off of him. She was already unbuttoning his shirt by the time Mark reached around her to tug the zipper down on her gown. Suzy unfastened his belt and his pants and playfully slipped her hand down the front of his underwear. She began to caress and stroke, feeling him gradually harden in her hand. Mark had just pushed her strapless dress down when he stopped and looked at her.

"Young lady," he said, putting on a stern and very proper-sounding English accent, "I believe that you have your hand down my pants."

"Whaddaya gonna do about it?" she responded with a New York accent.

"Well," he replied, staying in character, "it would seem that I have but two options. One, I could allow you to proceed along this present course of action, which would require me, ultimately, to change my skivvies. Or two, I could take them off now and have at you in my altogether."

Grinning, Suzy didn't wait for him to decide. She yanked his pants and underwear down and they joined her dress in a heap on the floor. It didn't take either of them long to divest themselves of the remaining pieces of clothing. Mark picked her up again and carried her the rest of the way to the bed.

Despite the rushed and impatient start, their lovemaking that evening was sweet and unhurried, as if they had all the time in the world.

Suzy brushed a tear away as she lay wearily on the hotel bed.

"Oh, Mark," she said under her breath, "I have to let you go." She closed her eyes and sighed. "So why is it so hard? You've been gone for three years, but you're still holding on to me so tightly." As she nodded off, she corrected her thought. "I suppose I'm the one holding on to you."

By now, though, she was asleep.

s soon as Fin opened his eyes, he knew something was wrong. His body felt strangely inert, as if his arms and legs had been tied down. His room was fairly dark, but was dimly illuminated by the lights on the monitor by his bed and various other little power display lights around the room.

The pain suddenly arrived along with the realization of what was wrong. He turned his head to the left and saw, to his horror, that his arm was missing. His sheet and hospital gown were dark with blood, and he quickly turned to the right to find similar results. Both of his arms had been tossed on the floor, lying in a widening pool of blood, and they were quickly joined by a leg, the cast clattering loudly on the tile floor.

Panting from the pain, tears streaming down his face, Fin arduously lifted his head and saw Peter, the physician's assistant, at the foot of his bed. His face, arms and scrubs were soaked with gore, and he had what looked like a big chef's knife in his hand, the blade and handle smeared and dripping with Fin's blood.

"Well, look who's awake!" he said with a friendly smile and a cheerful tone. "How are you feeling?"

"What the fuck are you doing to me?" Fin screamed, ignoring Peter question.

"Oh, Fin, honey, I'm so sorry, I was wrong. It *will* cost you an arm and a leg. And, well, the broken ones are useless to us, so I guess I shouldn't have taken them." He put his hand up to his mouth in a gesture of embarrassment. "Oops. My mistake."

"You can't do this!" Fin screamed. The pain was unbearable, and he couldn't stop the tears from streaming down his face.

"Oh, just relax," Peter scolded. "You don't need these, do you? I'm just going to cut them right out of your life." He positioned himself beside Fin's left leg and looked up at him with a grin. "Here we go."

Fin screamed as he felt the knife cut through his skin and muscle, arterial blood spraying all over Peter. The PA looked up at Fin and smiled, blood running down his face, dripping from his chin.

Suddenly, the lights came on and Fin saw a nurse come running into his room. Despite the pain and distraction, he felt a measure of surprise that she was able to run to his bed without tripping on the pile of bloody appendages on the floor.

"What is it?" she asked, looking back and forth from Fin to his beeping monitor. "Are you in pain?"

Fin, nearly hyperventilating, looked at her.

"Are you serious?" he yelled incredulously at her. "Are you telling me you really can't see –" He stopped when he saw his right hand in front of him, raised in an imploring gesture.

He lifted his head and saw that his body was still relatively intact, the casts on his broken limbs notwithstanding. He exhaled a groan as he laid his head back down on his pillow.

§

"Oh my god!" Suzy said, squeezing Fin's hand, after he related the latest hallucination to her. He was tired, his face drawn and haggard.

"I know. And I have another session with Peter before lunch. I'm afraid I'm a little less enthusiastic about it now than I was yesterday."

"What do you want to do now?" Suzy asked. "Do you want to sleep?"

"Oh my god, I could never sleep now. I'm tired, but I'm so tense there's no way I could ever relax enough to drop off to sleep." He sighed. "I'd be interested in seeing more of Cole's story, if he can manage to keep his hallucinations out of it. I have enough of my own."

"Of course. I'll see if I can contact him." Suzy settled herself in her chair, making herself comfortable. "Hopefully I can calm him enough to get another coherent episode or two out of him."

# 30

John and Isabel Springer spent a fair amount of time away from the ranch. John had many business interests that took him into Denver for long stretches, or as far east as Washington D.C. and New York. While the house staff had a responsibility to keep the house in readiness, they had some free time as well.

Cole spent some of his time with his uncle, admiring Springer's fine Oldenburg horses, magnificent animals sixteen hands high. Other times he would wander alone around the ranch. It was easier to be alone with his sometimes unsettling thoughts than to be with others. Whatever his activities, though, he usually ended up under the windmill.

That's where they found him when Isabel arrived one evening.

"My husband is still busy out east," she told Cole after the other servants had dispersed to care for their duties. "He's always so busy, so serious!" She rolled her eyes and took a drink of her whiskey.

"I take it you don't care for that life, ma'am?" Cole asked, but then, he mentally kicked himself. According to the brief training that Uncle Rupert gave him, he was not to speak to the Springers unless they specifically asked him a question. Mrs. Springer didn't seem to mind, though.

"It's positively tedious!" Then, her face took on a stern look, and she pressed her finger familiarly against his chest. "I thought I told you not to call me that."

"I'm sorry?" Cole looked confused, but inside, he was afraid he knew what she was talking about.

"Call me Sassy," she said in an imploring tone, pressing her shoulder against him.

"But Mrs. Springer," he said, but her look stopped him in mid-sentence. "Yes, ma'am – Sassy."

"That's better," she smiled. "It'll be our little secret. I'll be Mrs. Springer or ma'am when others are around," she said with a somewhat annoyed tone, "but when it's just the two of us, I'm Sassy."

Cole nodded. He was trying to keep his composure, but he was feeling excited and conspiratorial, and so guilty! What she was *asking was just not done, at least not in good society, certainly not with a servant and the wife of his employer.*

*She looked him up and down for a moment, and she finished off the whiskey. She held the glass out to Cole.*

*"I'm going up to my room," she said. "Would you bring me a drink?" Cole took the glass from her.*

*"I'm sorry. Wouldn't you rather have Mr. Gordon do that? Or perhaps your maid?"*

*"No, Cole," she replied, tilting her head, looking at him from under half-opened eyelids, "I want you to do it. And bring one for yourself."*

§

*"Are you from around here?" Isabel asked as Cole sat stiffly in a chair, holding his untouched drink. She picked up a bottle of tonic from her nightstand and poured some of it into her whiskey. She seemed visibly relieved when she took a drink of it.*

*"No ma'am – I mean Sassy. I'm from Centralia, Illinois."*

*"No fooling? Why, we were practically neighbors. I'm from St. Louis." Cole nodded, more nervous than he had ever been in his life. Isabel sat on her bed – her bed! – leaning casually on one hand while gesturing with the hand holding her drink. "This is your first job as a footman, isn't it?"*

*Cole looked up at her in alarm.*

*"You can tell?"*

*"Keep your shirt on," she said easily, "it's no problem. I'm certainly no stickler for formality."*

*Cole exhaled nervously. He looked at the drink in his hand and took a long swallow.*

*"I studied up a little before I left home. Then, when I got here, Uncle Rupert tutored me a little, before you arrived."*

*"Uncle Rupert?"*

*"Rupert Coleman. He works with your husband's horses."*

*"Ah, the horses." Cole wasn't sure what her tone said about that. "And you've never done anything like this before?" she asked teasingly.*

*"No, ma'am." She raised an eyebrow at him. Cole drained his glass. "No, Sassy. My father's a minister and we had a small farm*

142

*where we grew our food. I mainly worked on the farm. I've taken
odd jobs at times, but never an official position like this."*

*"Well, if it's any consolation, I think you're doing swell!"*

*"Yeah?"*

*"Yeah. And I think you're swell, too."*

*"Thank you." Cole managed a nervous smile.*

*Isabel held her glass out.*

*"Be a dear and bring us a couple more drinks, will you?"*

§

Cole nervously poured the whiskey, always keeping an eye out
for others. It was a small staff but, for as grand as it was, it was
also a fairly small house, so there weren't many places for the other
servants to be. Fortunately, it was getting late, and the others were
probably in their rooms for the night.

Cole climbed the stairs, his eyes darting about, afraid he might
come face-to-face with Mr. Gordon or one of the other staff members. But he didn't see anyone, and he breathed a sigh of relief
when he reached Isabel's door, and a very different nervousness
took over.

He tapped quietly on the door.

"Come in," came Isabel's voice from inside. Cole opened the
door and went inside, closing the door behind him. Only then did
he realize that Isabel was in bed. Technically, she was covered by
the lacy gown she wore, but it was sleek and thin enough that,
rather than hiding her breasts, it accentuated them, clinging to the
curves.

Cole focused his attention on her face as he approached and held
the tray out toward her, dismayed at how much it was shaking.

"Oh my goodness, Cole," Isabel said, taking one of the drinks,
"you're shaking like a leaf!" She patted the bed beside her. "Sit
down, honey. You need to relax."

Cole wanted to retreat to his room or, at least, head back to the
chair he was in before. But she was so beautiful, so enticing. And
he could see her nipples through the diaphanous fabric of her
gown! His knees threatened to give out, and he sat heavily down
on the edge of the bed, grasping the other glass of whiskey before
it slid off the tray.

"Oh, you poor thing," Isabel said sympathetically, pressing her hand against his arm. "You're so nervous."

Cole took a deep breath to try to slow his breathing, and hoping it might help relax him, he took a long slug of whiskey. Happily, it did help. To his relief, he could feel the whiskey burning down his throat and warming him from the inside out, calming his nerves.

"Is that better?" Isabel asked, leaning up toward him. Cole nodded weakly and looked at her. She was inches away from him, her long hair tumbling back over her shoulders, her brown eyes peering deeply into his.

Cole couldn't help it. He glanced down at her breasts, rising and falling with her breathing as she watched him, obviously concerned about his well-being. His eyes traveled up over her porcelain shoulders, and back to her face, her lips parted, slightly curved into not quite a smile, but welcoming.

The room flickered, and Cole knew it wasn't the gas lighting. The walls quivered briefly, with flames beginning to lick up the wallpaper. He closed his eyes tightly, concentrating.

Hold on, he told himself, don't lose it.

Cautiously, he opened his eyes again, and she was there, beautiful and inviting, and she smiled at him. He was powerless. He leaned forward and kissed her. To his great relief, she didn't push him away.

§

Sometime during the night, Cole woke up and felt Isabel's hair against his face. Her naked body fit perfectly against his as she slept peacefully in front of him, his arm resting across her hip. He looked around groggily. They had never turned the lights down, and the room was still fully lit.

He knew he would be spending eternity in hell. That was certain. The memory of her body under his, her legs wrapped around him, her hands pulling him closer, was still deliciously tickling his memory, and another more accursed part of his body. That part was still pressed against her soft buttocks, and before it regained its surprising proportions of the previous night, Cole slowly turned away from her.

*He carefully rolled over and got out of bed, pulling his clothes on as quietly as possible. He picked up the tray and the two glasses, and turned the gas down, leaving Isabel in darkness, as he quietly opened the door and slipped out of her room.*

## 31

D amn!" Suzy said, looking at Fin as he caught his breath after the episode. "Aside from a few brief episodes depicting their deaths in the Edinburgh vaults, this is the first time I've experienced the life of a man. Since we feel what the spirit felt, I have to say that it's," she squirmed in her chair a little, "enlightening."

"That's not the word that comes to my mind at the moment," Fin replied, looking at Suzy with a decidedly sinful expression.

"You know," Suzy said in a conspiratorial tone, casting a quick glance toward the door, "I've been kind of pleasantly surprised by how much privacy we have in here. They pretty much leave you alone between the therapy sessions."

"Stop!" Fin said. "I don't need any encouragement for what I'm already thinking!"

Suzy smiled.

"Still, I'm glad nobody's come in here while we're in our trances."

"That you know of," Fin said. "It's not like we'd be aware of it if they did."

"True," Suzy replied, "but if they did, they'd probably still be here trying to revive us."

They were both silent for a few moments, lost in their thoughts of the episode.

After a few moments, the door opened and Peter swept grandly into the room as Suzy had come to expect. Fin, however, tensed up when he saw the physician's assistant. His memory of the amputation hallucination still fixed in his mind, he wasn't anxious to see him.

"Hey, buddy," Peter said when he saw the expression on Fin's face, "I understand you had a pretty gruesome hallucination this morning." Fin nodded his head. "Well, normally, I admit I'd be flattered to be in your dreams, but in this case, for your benefit, I'll try to keep a low profile."

Suzy and Fin both had their doubts concerning his ability to do that, but Fin tried to smile, to acknowledge that he knew the hallucination, and his reaction now, wasn't Peter fault.

"I'll be in the waiting room down the hall," Suzy said, gathering up her things.

"We'll be done by lunch time," Peter said.

"Sounds good." She looked at Fin. "This will give me some time to get back into your book. But I'll be back for lunch. Maybe then we can pick up where we left off."

# 32

From what others on the staff had told him, Cole understood that Isabel liked to go to parties whenever possible. Often it was at the Brown Palace hotel in Denver. In fact, Springer even kept a room rented at the hotel specifically for Isabel, so she would have a place to stay after late parties downtown. Sometimes she and John hosted parties at their Denver house, not too far away from there, at 930 Washington Street.

In the fall, when she decided to host a party at the ranch, it meant that they were all busy. Cole, as footman, paid special attention to the table settings. He was also enlisted to circulate through the crowd with drinks before dinner was served.

John was huddled with a group of local businessmen in the corner discussing some potential business venture. Their conversation seemed private except for the mounted head of a large buck that was eavesdropping from the wall over their shoulders.

Isabel flitted from one guest to another, imbibing a surprising amount of alcohol, while Arthur Pryor's Shine on Harvest Moon played on the Victrola.

Cole remembered the realization he had when he first met her, that Isabel was different from the photograph of her looking shy, proper and demure.

What an underestimate that had been!

She was magnetic! Cole moved about the room carrying his tray with drinks on it, but he couldn't keep his eyes off of her. She seemed younger than her thirty years, laughing, joking, flirting. Back in St. Louis, she had been known as The Butterfly, and the name suited her. Parties were definitely her domain.

Cole noticed that her glass was empty, and he worked his way through the crowd toward her. Isabel saw him approaching, and Cole smiled at her. Isabel placed her empty glass on his tray and took another without looking at his face. She was already laughing at something someone had said.

Cole hesitated, surprised at her cold shoulder. He didn't expect her to visit with him, or even to greet him. But a smile, a glance, some private recognition of the intimacy they had shared.

*He waited for a few moments longer, trying to think of what he should do. He thought he saw the briefest expression of alarm flicker across Isabel's face as he stood there, but then a buxom matron wearing an alarmingly low-cut evening gown took the last drink from his tray. He needed to get more.*

§

*"Cole, I couldn't very well cast a longing glance at you when I was surrounded by our friends."* Cole felt silly now as Isabel scolded him the next day when he confronted her in the dining room. *"These people notice things like that. I'd be raked over the coals in* The Post, *or worse, they'd tell John."*

*"I know,"* he replied sheepishly. *"It just felt like you were ashamed of me, or you were rejecting me. But you're right. I'm sorry. I don't want to get you in trouble."*

*"You're sweet,"* she replied, stroking his cheek softly. Cole felt something like a shiver at her touch. *"John's leaving for New York this afternoon."* She lowered her voice to a whisper. *"Come to my room tonight."*

*She allowed her hand to slip down to his chest, and Cole felt her finger slide deliciously down his belly. She turned away before it reached his belt, but he was still tingling from that tease as she left the room and climbed the stairs.*

*It was all he could do to keep his mind on his work that day. When he had the opportunity, after he had completed his afternoon duties, he went down to the windmill for a few minutes. The effect wasn't quite what he had hoped for.*

*With the coming of fall, the weather was cooling. Cole didn't mind that, but the wind and the grey sky today, rather than calming him, seemed to darken his mood. Following his earlier time in Isabel's bedroom, he had been tormented by guilt, but it had been an unintentional encounter. He hadn't known ahead of time that it was going to happen.*

*Today, he was anticipating another such encounter. And this time, it would not be unintentional. It was completely premeditated. He was not only coveting another man's wife, but he would be having illicit relations with her. He would be making improper use of his privy member, and he was looking forward to it!*

*The grey sky began turning dark, and he could already feel the flames of hell licking at his feet. Despite the eternal damnation awaiting him, though, he couldn't get his mind off of Isabel.*

§

*After John Springer departed to catch his train to New York, Isabel had requested a simple dinner. Mary, the cook, had made a delicious vegetable soup, and Cole served it to Isabel with fresh-baked bread and cheese. Isabel ate her solitary dinner while reading* The Vagabond, *the latest romance novel that had caught her interest.*

*Cole stood at the ready in case she needed anything. She didn't seem to notice his gaze traveling along the soft white curve of the back of her neck and her shoulders. His eyes couldn't go any further than the top of her dress, but his memory could. He remembered the curve of her back, and he longed to caress it again. He craved the warmth of her creamy body pressed against his.*

*He was startled out of his ruminations when Isabel closed her book and started pushing her chair back. He rushed forward to pull the chair for her.*

*"Thank you, Cole," she said as she stood up. "That will be all."*

*"Yes, ma'am," Cole replied. Isabel gave him a stern look, but it was immediately followed by the beginnings of a smile. She left the dining room as Cole cleared the table.*

*After the dining room was neatened up, Cole spent a few quiet moments in the small staff dining room. The others were talking, but he wasn't aware of them. He ate his soup in silence, then excused himself.*

*Another hour or so passed before Cole was certain that the rest of the staff had settled in their rooms for the night. After making certain nobody was around, he stealthily made his way to Isabel's room. He put his head to her door and listened for a moment, to make sure nobody else was in there with her. It wouldn't do to be found out by Irma, Isabel's maid, or someone else on the staff.*

*He tapped lightly on the door, and it opened a few seconds later. Isabel smiled at him and held the door open for him. She was wearing a flimsy dressing gown, and Cole noticed it was steamy in her room.*

150

*"I've drawn us a bath," Isabel said, as if it was the most natural thing in the world. She grabbed his lapel and pulled him into the room, closing the door behind him. As she tugged his jacket off of him, he hoped that the water in the bath tub would be enough to douse the hellfire and brimstone that he knew were waiting for him.*

*But he had his doubts.*

§

*His business in New York done, Springer returned to the ranch for a while, before he and Isabel left for their winter home in Pasadena, California. While they wintered there, Cole had more time to himself each day, once his duties were completed.*

*And he hated it.*

*He couldn't get Isabel out of his mind. She was the most beautiful, enchanting woman he had ever known. Even Laura was fading into the background of his memory. He felt conflicted about that, too. The things he had done with Laura had been wrong. He had committed fornication, but at least it had not been adultery. Still, he had felt a certain loyalty to her.*

*But Isabel! To have spent such intimate moments with her, and now, to have her snatched suddenly from his life for the next few months seemed the ultimate cruelty, and it was just too hard to bear. He spent more time than usual at the windmill, trying to calm himself.*

*Since memories of Isabel predominated his thoughts, most times, his attempts at calmness resulted in little more than watching the flames of hell creep ever closer.*

## 33

Winter in Colorado, Cole quickly noticed, can be a diverse mix of unseasonably warm and sunny, and blisteringly cold, grey and snowy, with varying degrees in between. He couldn't blame the Springers for spending the winter in southern California.

That realization didn't make those months pass any easier for him.

If the weather was tolerable, he spent a fair amount of his free time, after completing his duties in the house, at the windmill, wandering around the grounds, or visiting with his uncle, watching him work with the horses. He made it a point to not even hint to Uncle Rupert about the intimate time he had spent with Isabel. He didn't want that getting back to his father.

If the weather was bad, he spent a good deal of time in his room, sometimes reading his Bible, but studiously avoiding The Song of Solomon. Being where he was most comfortable, and insulated from the rest of the staff, helped keep the bad humors at bay. When they came anyway, being in his room at least kept them from the view of others.

When the Springers returned, Cole was ecstatic, despite the fact that he couldn't spend any time alone with Isabel. With Springer there, they had to be so much more careful.

Isabel seemed very adept at keeping it a secret. Cole, however, found it to be quite a struggle to prevent himself from addressing Isabel and requesting time with her. There were times he was sure that Springer had noticed him watching Isabel, and he resolved to be more disciplined, for his and Isabel's sake.

§

In March, a new friend of John Springer's appeared at the ranch. Harold Francis Henwood was a tall, good-looking man, younger than Springer and impeccably-dressed.

Isabel seemed to take notice.

Cole, noting her attention directed to Henwood, took a position outside the living room, but where he could keep an eye on the situation.

"I don't know, Frank," Springer was saying, "I'm not sure I want to tie up any money in this Blau gas."

"If the American Blau Gas Company does decide to build a plant in Denver, as they're considering," Henwood advised his friend, "you'll be getting in on the ground floor. Blau gas is the fuel of the future."

"I'm not so sure. We're getting electric lights installed here. Electricity, now that's the fuel of the future."

"Imagine," Isabel contributed, "just touching a button on the wall and the lights are instantly on."

"Yes, but electricity still needs to be generated," Henwood replied. Isabel seemed disappointed that her comment didn't derail the talk of business. She went to a nearby cabinet and began pouring drinks. "And besides," Henwood continued, "not everyone has your resources, John. The general public won't be able to afford electricity. And they'll still need to heat their homes."

"Which is why I think I'm leaning toward propane."

"Propane?"

"It was discovered by a Frenchman about fifty years ago, and it's going to be available as a fuel here in America very soon, possibly this year. And it's much less expensive to produce because it's simply a by-product of petroleum refinement."

"Oh, must you always be talking business, John?" Isabel said, exasperated, handing a glass to John and one to Henwood.

"I'm sorry, Sassy," Henwood chuckled, "I'm afraid I'm the culprit. I'm the one who started trying to separate John from his money."

Cole bristled inwardly at Henwood's use of Isabel's pet name. He watched for a while, noticing Isabel's flirting with Henwood, and Springer's apparent blindness to it. There were a couple of times that Springer made a comment about their earlier discussion concerning Blau gas versus propane, but Isabel would have none of it.

Though Henwood easily engaged in conversation with both Springers, he seemed completely taken with Isabel. His mood darkening, Cole left a few times to fulfil his duties, but he returned to his position a couple of times to monitor the situation.

*As they laughed and visited into the night, Springer suggested that Henwood spend the night rather than venturing out in the dark. Cole turned in a huff and went to his room.*

## 34

After lunch, Fin was paid a visit by a physical therapist who took him from his room for a session of working his arm and leg.

When the session was finished, he was wheeled back into his room and helped into his bed as Suzy smiled at him from her chair. The therapist left a crutch leaning against the wall beside his bed, as he was expected to get up and move around rather than stay in bed.

"What are you smiling about?" he asked after the therapist left.

"I'm just happy to see you again," Suzy said.

"Yeah?" Fin replied, grinning. "You're totally besotted with me, aren't you?"

"I suppose I seem to tolerate you reasonably well," Suzy replied, donning her smartass persona at the last possible moment.

"Mm hmm," Fin said, feeling a boost in his confidence despite the intense fatigue he felt. His lack of sleep, followed by his therapy sessions were weighing on him, and the exhaustion was showing on his face.

As he slipped into a nap, Suzy let him sleep.

§

When he opened his eyes again, Suzy was still sitting there, reading. Fin was happy to see that she seemed to be completely engrossed in his book, but her reading was interrupted when Dr. Ivanov entered the room.

"Ah, Ms. Queenn," he said quietly, approaching the back of her chair, "I am so glad you are here."

"Why is that?" Suzy asked.

"You are very beautiful woman. I am attracted to you very much."

Fin bunched his eyebrows together, not only at his doctor's inappropriate behavior, but especially at Suzy's smile in response.

"That's so sweet of you, Doctor," she replied. "Thank you."

"Ees nothing," Dr. Ivanov said as he touched her shoulder softly. To Fin's horror, Ivanov slipped his hand down from there, into Suzy's blouse. Fin couldn't see his hand at that point, but from its position, he knew it was cupped over Suzy's breast.

Fin felt as if his heart stopped in his chest. Instead of fighting Ivanov off, Suzy smiled and pressed her hand against his, crushing it hard against her breast. As he squeezed it, Suzy moaned. She reached up with her other hand and cupped it around Ivanov's neck, pulling him down to her, and she kissed him hard.

Getting past his shock, Fin finally found his voice and spoke up.

"Suzy," he said, his voice cracking with emotion, "what – what are you doing?"

"Come on, Fin," she replied derisively, "you're a broken man. Dr. Ivanov is whole and strong and virile."

Ivanov looked at Fin and smiled. As he was bending over Suzy, he decided that he was in a better position to hold her other breast. As he moved his hand, Suzy turned into it a little, facilitating his grasp.

As Fin felt the tears welling up, he felt pressure on his arm. He blinked back the tears, and Dr. Ivanov was gone. Suzy wasn't in her chair anymore. She was standing beside Fin's bed, holding his arm, her face expressing worry.

"What's wrong, baby?" she asked. The moment he realized that it had been another hallucination, the tears gushed and he reached up with his right arm and pulled Suzy down to him, holding her tightly.

Suzy held onto him, taking her cues from him. After a couple of minutes, he relaxed his grip and wiped the tears away.

"Another hallucination?" she asked, as she straightened up.

"Yeah, thank god," Fin replied. He wiped the tears away as Suzy frowned, confused at his response. "Why can't I ever have a pleasant hallucination?" he sighed.

He suddenly remembered the one he experienced a couple of mornings ago back at the hospital.

"Actually," he corrected himself, "I guess there was that one."

"What was it?" Suzy asked.

"Never mind."

He took a deep breath to try to clear his head. He blew it out and looked up at Suzy.

"Can we finish this guy's story and send him on his way out of this snake pit?"

"This guy?" Suzy asked. "You mean Cole?"

"Yeah," Fin replied, rubbing his face roughly.

"What did you mean by 'snake pit'?"

"Oh, it's from an old movie with Olivia de Havilland in an insane asylum."

"Ah. We could try to send him on now, if you want."

"Well," Fin said a little sheepishly, "I'm curious about how his story ends."

Suzy smiled and pulled her chair closer to Fin's bed. Holding his hand, she initiated contact with Cole to begin another episode.

## 35

Frank Henwood became a frequent visitor at the Cross Country Ranch, sometimes even when Springer wasn't there. To Cole's chagrin, Isabel used the time when Springer was gone to become more intimate with Henwood instead of with Cole. When Isabel wasn't there, he suspected that she was in her room at the Brown Palace.

With Henwood.

Weeks passed, and Cole had little contact with Isabel, other than what contact was called for in his duties in the house. She seemed happiest when Henwood was around, but almost despondent at other times.

Whenever possible, when Henwood was there, Cole took positions out of their sight in order to keep an eye on them and, he hoped, to determine what was bothering Isabel. One day in May, the situation came to a head.

§

"Honey, I'm worried about you," Henwood said to Isabel, the endearment causing Cole to scowl outside the doorway of the room where he had stationed himself. He had a cloth in his hand for polishing silver nearby, in case anybody came along and wondered why he was there.

"Whatever for, Frank?" Isabel asked, pacing back and forth near the chair where Henwood sat.

"You just don't seem like yourself lately. You seem unhappy about something. It's not John, is it?"

"No," Isabel waved her hand dismissively. "Nothing like that."

"Then what is it, my dear?"

Isabel pushed the fingers of both hands into her abundant hair and massaged her scalp for a few moments, trying to ease a headache. She looked at Henwood, then seemed resigned to telling him what was on her mind.

"There's a man I've known for a while," she sighed. "I was," she seemed to flush a bit, "well, I was involved with him before I met John. A few months ago, I was in St. Louis, and I happened upon him again, and we seemed to pick up where we left off."

*Watching through the space between the door and the door jamb, Cole saw Henwood stiffen up a bit.*

*"You're – you're intimate with this man?"*

*"I was," Isabel admitted. "And I, well, I'm afraid I penned some rather foolish little letters to him. Mind you," she was quick to add, "this was before I met you."*

*"I'm not worried," Henwood smiled, but he became serious again. "So, does John know about this man?"*

*"He knows that Tony and I have been friends for years, but beyond that, no, he knows nothing of our relationship."*

*"Tony, eh?"*

*"Yes, Tony von Phul."*

*Cole knew the name. He remembered reading newspaper articles in the Midwest about his exploits, racing horses and cars, and as a balloonist. He knew he was also a favorite with the women.*

*"Von Fool?" Henwood said sardonically, raising his right eyebrow at her.*

*"Yes, well, he's a little more shrewd than his name might imply," Isabel smirked.*

*"So tell me, what's the problem, dear?" He leaned forward in the chair, encouraging her to continue.*

*Isabel took a deep breath and sighed, resuming her pacing.*

*"He's threatening to show these letters to John and reveal my infidelity unless I resume our relationship."*

*"He's coming here?" Henwood asked, sitting upright.*

*"He is. He shall be in Denver next week. He means to meet me at the Brown Palace next Wednesday to formally make his demands."*

*"But he must be stopped, my dear!" Henwood said sitting forward, impulsively reaching out and grasping Isabel about the hips and turning her toward him, effectively putting a stop to her pacing. "John can't know about this!"*

*"I agree."*

*"It would positively ruin you. And John," he added as an afterthought. Isabel placed her hands on his shoulders.*

*"And by putting me in an unfavorable light," she added, "it could also hinder our own clandestine romance."*

"Yes, well, there is that, too," Henwood smiled, looking up at her and hugging her body tightly against him. "So, dear Isabel, let me meet with him. I'll get the letters from him and send the bounder on his way."

"You're very sweet to offer," she said, looking down at him affectionately, and placing a hand upon his cheek. Henwood looked up at Isabel like a devoted puppy, willing to do anything for her approval. "But I feel I should deal with this myself."

"Isabel, John will be back in town on Saturday. Von Phul will be here on Wednesday. How do you mean to be able to handle the situation?"

"I'll think of something."

Suddenly, Isabel gasped and abruptly pushed his shoulders back. Henwood quickly removed his hands from her hips.

Cole moved a bit to try to see what had happened, and there was Cora, the housekeeper. She had entered the room from the other side, surprising the couple, and surprising herself at least as much.

Isabel stuttered out some kind of excuse, and in the end, didn't appear any less guilty than before.

"My apologies, ma'am," Cora mumbled as she bobbed a quick curtsy and left.

"So much for our clandestine romance," Henwood mumbled.

§

Henwood spent the night, supposedly in a guest room, but Cole knew that the room was connected to Isabel's by a shared bathroom. And he noticed that Irma, Isabel's maid, made several trips to Isabel's room with drinks that evening. That in itself was not unusual. Isabel drank quite a lot. What Cole noticed was that the tray holding two glasses was frequently delivered only to Isabel's room, and never to Henwood's.

By the next morning, Cole had gotten no sleep at all, and was struggling to keep his demons at bay. After Isabel had said goodbye to Henwood, Cole met him at the door with his hat and overcoat.

"If I may be so bold, sir," he said quietly, "I am aware of Mrs. Springer's dilemma with Mr. von Phul. I also know of your devotion to Mrs. Springer." Henwood looked at Cole with what he

160

probably hoped was an offended expression, but really just looked guilty and, Cole hoped, afraid. Cole steeled himself for what came next. "I know of Mr. von Phul's exploits," he said, "and that he is known as a violent man. I would suggest, sir, that if you were to confront him, it might be in your best interests if you were armed."

"I've never owned a weapon in my life," Henwood replied in an offended tone. "I've always felt that people who rely on guns are cowards."

"Nevertheless, sir, under the circumstances, it might be wise."

Draping the overcoat over his arm, Henwood took the hat and tapped it on his head. Glancing over his shoulder to where he had last seen Isabel, he sighed and nodded his head toward Cole.

"Thank you."

Cole nodded back and opened the door for him. As he watched Henwood walk down the steps toward his automobile, he wondered about the fate awaiting himself.

What he had told Henwood had been correct. Tony von Phul was known to be an impetuous daredevil type, and that he was known, often, to carry a revolver.

Cole cared nothing about Henwood's safety. The warning was not for that purpose. But during the night, as he lay awake in torment, he had wondered about the possibility of initiating an event that might simultaneously rid him of both rivals. What were the chances that they might end up shooting each other?

It occurred to him that he seemed a little like King David in the Bible. David manipulated events in the battle with the Ammonites to cause the death of Uriah the Hittite, so that he could have Uriah's wife, Bathsheba, who by this time was already pregnant by David.

There were obvious differences, of course. Cole was no king, Henwood was no soldier, and Isabel was not pregnant. And, of course, there was no way that Cole could manipulate Henwood's or von Phul's behavior. But the actions he was taking, and the hoped-for outcome, struck him as similar.

He sighed as he saw the flames blazing across the prairie, racing toward the house. Cole quickly closed the door.

§

Isabel was so distracted by the Tony von Phul debacle that when Cole had any time alone in her presence, she wouldn't give him the time of day. When she wasn't there, Cole knew, she was most likely staying in her suite at the Brown Palace. He didn't like to think who might be there with her.

On Saturday, Springer returned home from his business trip, and in the following days, he and Isabel engaged in several activities away from the ranch.

Cole's agitation was never-ending. When the Springers were there, his hands frequently shook when serving them, threatening to bring their unwanted negative attention upon him. When they were away, when he wasn't imagining Henwood's or von Phul's hands on Isabel, he was seeing a grim and torturous eternity in hell for himself.

On Tuesday, the Springers had dinner at the Brown Palace, and had spent the night there. On Wednesday, after Springer left for his office, Isabel arrived back at the ranch.

With Tony von Phul.

The man had an athletic build and seemed to wear a permanent expression of self-confidence. The expression seemed to go very well with his swagger.

Cole's agitation was now tinged with astonishment. He couldn't fathom why Isabel would bring the man blackmailing her to her home. She showed von Phul around, whether to show off her situation or to, somehow, appeal to his sense of goodwill, Cole didn't know. He was glad to see, though, that they never went into her bedroom.

§

Cole was busily polishing a silver tray on display in the dining room, and he didn't hear Isabel approach.

"Cole," she said, and Cole started, turning quickly to face her, "do you know how to drive an automobile?"

"Yes, ma'am," he said, quickly recovering. "One of the jobs I had back in Centralia was as a deliveryman."

"Wonderful!" Isabel said with an obvious sense of relief. "I'm afraid Mr. Lepar has taken ill."

162

*Cole had noticed that Thomas Lepar, the chauffeur, had seemed a little green when he came in after bringing Isabel and von Phul to the ranch that morning. He had retired to his room.*

*"Would you be able to take us back?" she asked.*

*"Of course," Cole replied, trying not to sound too eager. It would be strange, but he would be with Isabel.*

*"Thank you, Cole," Isabel said, placing her hand on his arm. In the brief moment she touched him, he remembered the times he had spent in her arms, in her bed, and it almost brought tears to his eyes. "Take whatever you'll need for the night. You'll stay at our house on Washington Street. Mr. Springer and I will be going to the theater tonight. We'll telephone in the morning when we need you."*

## 36

The drive up into Denver had, as Cole expected, been strange. Isabel and von Phul had spoken quietly in the back seat as Cole drove, but too quietly for Cole to hear any of it. He dropped von Phul off at the Brown Palace, noting his admonishing expression aimed at Isabel. After that, Isabel directed Cole to their house at 930 Washington Street. It was a lovely house, with brick arches at the front porch and a carriage house in back. After a brief orientation, she had him take her back to the Brown Palace.

Cole was disappointed that Isabel had been so businesslike the entire time. Being alone with her, he couldn't help remembering their time together at the ranch, their intimacies in her bed. He remembered the smell of her skin and her hair, the softness of her body, the taste of her lips and tongue, the delicious pressure of his body against the cushion of her breasts. He tingled as he recalled the feel of her hands touching and holding parts of him that nobody had ever touched before.

Well, one person had. After those brief moments behind the shed in Centralia, Cole had hoped to get some more time alone with Laura. He got his wish a couple of weeks later.

Laura played the piano, though she didn't own one, and she played music that Cole wasn't allowed to listen to. She played the kind of music that Cole's father said appealed to man's sinful, carnal desires.

Cole was becoming familiar with those desires, whether he wanted to or not. One day, Laura came over when his parents were gone, and she excitedly asked if he wanted to hear the latest music she had gotten. Cole readily agreed.

Laura sat down at his mother's piano, studying the music in front of her for a few seconds, flexing her fingers, then she took a deep breath. Suddenly, her hands started flying over the keys, playing something called The Maple Leaf Rag by Scott Joplin.

As he watched her hands bouncing back and forth over the keyboard, Cole was astounded that she could keep track of the keys she was striking so quickly. And admittedly, Laura didn't play the song perfectly, but well enough that Cole could feel a sensation of excitement building inside him. He didn't think it had anything to do with sinful, carnal desires, but he loved the music.

"Wow!" Cole exclaimed when she finished. "That was killer!"

"Thanks," Laura said, smiling shyly, blushing. Cole was intrigued by that apparent shyness, after she had so easily gotten partly undressed in front of him.

"I'm serious," he said, "I've never heard anything like that!"

"Yeah, Scott Joplin's amazing."

"You're amazing," Cole said, blushing a little himself.

Laura got up off the piano stool and sat down next to Cole on the settee, leaning against him comfortably. Remembering how she had leaned on his thigh a couple of weeks before, Cole put his hand on her thigh lightly, almost experimentally. His hand tingled with the feel of the warmth of her leg through the cotton fabric. Laura placed her hand on top of his, and she looked up at him, leaning forward to kiss him.

Feeling her lips warm and soft against his, Cole's breathing quickened. Laura's hand traveled up his arm, finding its way to his face, and she pulled him harder against her, opening her mouth. He followed her example and opened his, as well. When their tongues touched, Cole felt a sudden surge in his groin as his privy member quickly hardened.

Cole gasped and Laura pulled away to look at him. Somehow, she seemed to understand why he gasped, and she looked down. She could see the bulge in his trousers, and she moved her hand down to touch it. Cole felt a thrill unlike any he had ever experienced before. Nobody had ever touched him there.

"We shouldn't be doing this," he whispered, at the same time hoping Laura would continue. He knew God was not happy about them doing such things which were reserved for a husband and wife.

He remembered the story of Joseph and Potiphar's wife, and how Joseph had been able to pull himself away from her seductions, even though her lies about it to her husband afterward meant years in prison for Joseph. Now, with Laura's hand on his crotch, Cole knew he didn't possess anywhere near the amount of self-control that Joseph had.

*Feeling his breaths coming faster, Cole leaned again into Laura and placed his hand gingerly on her breast. She moaned and moved the rest of the distance to Cole and kissed him again, her hand moving up and down on him.*

*They were saved from committing mortal sin when they heard Cole's parents coming in the front door. As she had behind the shed, Laura laughed as she got up and went back to her original position on the piano stool, greeting his parents when they came in the room.*

*The memory lingered pleasantly in his mind as he came to a stop at the entrance to the Brown Palace. Cole got out of the automobile and opened the door for Isabel, taking her hand to help her out.*

*He held on a little longer than was necessary.*

*"John and I shall dine here at the hotel," Isabel said, "then we will be going to see the Ziegfeld Follies across the street at the Broadway Theater. We likely won't be needing you tonight, but please remain at the ready, just in case."*

*"Yes, ma'am," Cole said. He was disappointed that she didn't cast a scolding glance at him for not calling her Sassy. He watched her until she disappeared into the Brown Palace.*

*Hearing a thunderous noise, he looked back down Broadway, and saw Springer's prize Oldenburg horses stampeding toward him. It was something he had seen several times before, with some variations. This time, the horses were on fire, as if they were bringing the blazes of hell directly to him.*

*Hoping he could somehow escape that fate, he sighed and got back into the motor car, waiting for the stampede to pass him by. When the horses never reached the automobile, Cole started it up, driving himself back to their house on Washington Street.*

## 37

After another round of migraine therapy consultations with Peter, it was almost dinner time. Fin had arranged for Suzy to have dinner with him. But before their dinners arrived, Suzy accompanied Fin down the hallway and back as he followed through on moving around as the physical therapist had suggested.

"This is harder than I would have thought," Fin said as he hobbled along. "I sprained my ankle pretty badly when I was a teenager and had to use crutches for a while. But I had two good arms and used both crutches. That was easy compared to this."

"Well," Suzy encouraged, "I think you're already doing better than you were when you started just a few minutes ago."

"Thanks." Fin wasn't so sure about that, but he appreciated the support.

He suddenly stiffened up and froze as he heard a hissing sound beside him. He looked down to his side and saw a snake coiled up against the wall. At the same time, he heard the distinctive sound of a rattlesnake on the right. As he looked around, he saw others, as well, and his fear and a compounded lack of sleep caused him to hold his breath.

The snakes of various sizes and levels of aggression were writhing on the floor, some right against his feet. He lifted his right leg, the one in the cast, but he was still terrified by the coral snakes squirming around his left foot.

"What is it?" Suzy asked, squeezing his arm. Fin started at her touch, but he looked at her face, peering up at him. She seemed unconcerned.

"Do you see any snakes around us?" Fin asked shakily.

"Snakes?" Suzy echoed, looking around. "No."

With a sense of relief, Fin exhaled his breath, but he felt tears come to his eyes with the knowledge that he was the victim of yet another hallucination.

"Goddamn it!" he said, closing his eyes and feeling the tears tumble down his cheeks. "I just had to mention *The Snake Pit*.

"Come on, honey," Suzy said, taking charge, "we're fine." She put her arm around him and guided him back toward his room, just as an orderly arrived with their dinners.

"After dinner," Fin said after the orderly left them alone, "let's see if we can finish this fucktangled story and be done with it."

## 38

Cole sat at a table in the Wine Room of the Brown Palace. He had gone back to the house on Washington Street, but he had been restless. His mind was being tortured by memories of his time with Isabel, in addition to the events he had hoped to set in motion with Henwood and von Phul. He couldn't sleep, and he decided, impulsively, to come back to the Brown Palace.

Here in this bar on the Broadway side of the building, he imagined that he might actually be able to see Isabel tonight, if she and her husband happened to stop in here for a drink after the show. The Wine Room, or The Marble Bar as it was known for the beautiful gold onyx-topped bar, was filling up. Cole noticed that a lot of people were coming in, as he had suspected, after the Broadway Theater let out.

At the bar, Cole saw somebody who didn't seem to fit in with the others lined up there. Among the men in suits and bowler hats stood a man in dusty-looking clothes, a high-crowned hat with a wide brim, and chaps.

Nobody else seemed to pay him any mind, but as Cole was watching him, it seemed to catch the man's attention. The man strolled over toward Cole, taking off his hat as he approached. He had grey hair, somewhat droopy eyelids and a fractious mustache, and eyebrows to match.

"Good evening, son," the man smiled. "Alright if I join you?"

Cole would have rather been alone, but he didn't want to be rude. He nodded his head, and the man sat down in the chair opposite him, leaning back comfortably.

"What's your name?"

"Cole."

"Nice to meet you, Cole. I'm Henry." Cole nodded again and took a sip of his whiskey.

"If you don't mind my saying so, sir," Cole said, "you don't strike me as someone who would frequent a place like this."

Henry grinned, looking down at his clothes.

"You're not the first one to tell me that. I was dressed very much like this some years back when I walked into the Windsor

Hotel, over on Eighteenth and Larimer. I was told I had to leave. They had a very sophisticated dress code."

Cole nodded noncommittally, not sure what to do with the information. The man's story didn't seem that interesting to him.

"They didn't know I was one of the richest men in Colorado."

"You are?" Cole asked, thinking the story just got a little more interesting.

"Well, not now. But I made myself two or three fortunes during my life."

"So, what did you do?"

"I wasn't one to make a public spectacle of myself, so I left. But I got my revenge. A few years later, I built this hotel. Finer than the Windsor in every way."

"You built the Brown Palace?"

"Henry Brown, at your service."

"But," Cole said, wrinkling his eyebrows in thought, "I thought the man that built this hotel died a few years ago."

Henry looked at Cole, the mirth disappearing from his face, and vanished.

Cole jumped, realizing that it had happened again. It had always unnerved him, back in Centralia, when he made contact with someone who had passed on. And it wasn't just the fact that he had spoken with someone who was dead, but that it was strictly forbidden.

> There shall not be found among you any one
> that maketh his son or his daughter to pass through
> the fire, or that useth divination, or an observer of
> times, or an enchanter, or a witch, or a charmer, or
> a consulter with familiar spirits, or a wizard, or a
> necromancer. For all that do these things are an
> abomination unto the LORD.

It had been quite a while since it had happened, and frankly, Cole hadn't missed it. But now that a ghost had just sat across from him, visiting pleasantly with him, he could feel how tenuous his hold on sanity was.

*The Wine Room started shaking, the tables and glasses rattling – in his mind, anyway. Glancing around, he saw that nobody else seemed to notice. Cole saw the hellfire begin its flickering in his peripheral vision, and he closed his eyes tightly, panting for breath, trying to keep the fire at bay. He cautiously opened his eyes and picked up his glass, draining the last of his whiskey.*

*As the whiskey burned its way down his throat, Cole took a deep breath, feeling a little more relaxed. He sighed and sat back in his chair, when suddenly, he heard the explosive sound of a gun shot up near the bar.*

*Cole started, looking toward the source of the sound, and he was surprised to see Frank Henwood on one knee, pointing a pistol at Tony von Phul. People were scattering in all directions, fleeing the area in a panic, as four more shots were fired in quick succession. After that, Henwood kept squeezing the trigger, but the hammer only clicked against the spent shells.*

*White smoke rose over the bar and swirled in the currents of air from the fleeing people. As the smell of burnt gunpowder drifted toward him, Cole saw von Phul among those who had fallen to the floor, along with a couple of other men, one of them shot in the leg. A man grabbed the empty gun from Henwood's hand and put it on the bar, but oddly, nobody tried to restrain Henwood. He stood up, then turned to his side and bent down to pick up his straw hat which had fallen on the floor.*

*He approached the man he had shot in the leg and said something that Cole couldn't hear, and the man responded angrily. Henwood seemed surprised to be addressed in such a way and, fumbling his hat in his hands, he walked toward the door into the lobby of the hotel.*

*As the bartender was already on the telephone calling for an ambulance, a policeman rushed in the doorway from the street, apparently alerted by the sound of the shots. He quickly questioned several gathered around the bar, and several of them pointed to the doorway where Henwood had disappeared.*

*A couple of people assisted von Phul to his feet, a blood-soaked handkerchief wrapped around his wrist, and helped him into his coat. He seemed weak, but Cole was, in light of his recent feelings of guilt and remorse, happy to see that he was not dead. Henwood's apparent unfamiliarity with guns had evidently averted any loss of life.*

*Still, intentions were more important than unexpected outcomes. Cole's hoped-for intentions had been for both men to be taken out of his way so that he could engage in his adulterous relationship with Isabel.*

*All at once, the tables and chairs, the walls, and all the people around him erupted in flames. There was a momentary collective scream from the people until, a second or two later, they all dropped to the floor. The bottles of alcohol lined up behind the bar exploded, sending burning glass shards in all directions, adding to the holocaust. In an instant, the Wine Room was transformed into a deafening cacophony of hissing and crackling tinder.*

*Cole sat amidst the conflagration, watching his skin char, knowing that it was entirely deserved.*

## 39

Suzy emerged quickly from the episode, her eyes wide with panic. She was panting and brushing her arms in a frenzy until she realized that the fire had just been yet another hallucination.

"God, I don't think I can take much more of this guy's story," she said breathlessly. She looked up at Fin and saw that his eyes were glassy, probably, she thought, from the strain of the mental agony and guilt that were being reinforced by Cole's episodes.

She became concerned by his expression, a sort of sad hopelessness, and she knew his exhaustion wasn't helping, either.

"Fin," she said, "I think you need to get some sleep."

"After that?" Fin replied. "I think it's going to be a while before sleep becomes possible."

"Well, maybe they can give you something to help you out."

"Yeah, and next thing I know, I'm addicted to sleeping pills."

"Honey, it doesn't work that way," Suzy said, reaching for his hand. He jumped when he felt her touch, but he calmed a bit when she wrapped her fingers around his. "And this is the perfect place for it. Treating addictions and dependencies is one of the things they specialize in here. They're not going to do anything that would *cause* you to become addicted."

Fin took a deep breath and looked at Suzy through a fog, as if it was difficult to think. Finally, he nodded in agreement.

"Okay, baby," Suzy said, squeezing his hand. She started gathering up her things. "I'm going to go back to my hotel and let you get some rest. On my way out, I'll ask them about giving you something to help you sleep." Fin nodded again.

Suzy slung her purse over her shoulder and she stopped and looked at Fin. "I love you, honey," she said.

"I love you, too, Suzy," Fin replied, the warmth returning to his voice, at least momentarily.

It was only a couple of minutes after Suzy left that Peter swept into his room (Fin briefly wondered where he got his energy) and handed him a little cup with a pill in it and a cup of water.

Five minutes after that, Fin was asleep.

§

Fin slept through the night, uninterrupted, dreamless sleep, and he awoke feeling somewhat refreshed. It was early, though, and he didn't feel like he could go back to sleep.

With Cole's feelings of guilt fresh in his mind, Fin remembered his parents' visit three days before. Within just a few moments, his own guilt resurfaced again, and he thought about everything he had given up.

The religious belief system wasn't high on the list. He had never really connected with that anyway. It had never been in his heart. But he missed his family. He missed some of the friends that he had lost. As Suzy would have said, though, what kind of friends could they be if they weren't his friends anymore just because he had decided the religion wasn't right for him?

But the beliefs were still there, to some extent. It was what he had been raised with, and even if he was no longer sure about it, they still lingered as question marks in the back of his mind.

He still noticed things that he was sure they would point to as scriptural proof that 'the end was near.' Having turned his back on those beliefs, that way of life, was he now destined for the eternal punishment that they believed in?

Thinking about it made his head hurt, and since that reminded him of his migraines, he decided he wanted to think about something else. He wanted a distraction.

174

He remembered what Suzy had told him about how she initiated the episodes, how she relaxed and opened her mind, sending out a sort of mental greeting to the obliging spirit.

Within moments, the next episode began.

## 40

Cole could scarcely believe it. Everyone was talking about it. Almost twelve hours after Henwood shot him, Tony von Phul died. The wound in his wrist hadn't been the only one. There were two others. Another bullet had entered his back, in his shoulder, and the final shot, the one that proved his undoing, entered his side, doing untold damage as it passed through his body.

Not only that, but one of the other men who had been shot in the Wine Room, standing at the Marble Bar, a George Copeland, had also died.

Cole knew that it was his fault. If he hadn't recommended to Henwood that he arm himself, this would not have happened. It's true that von Phul had been known to carry a weapon, though one had not been found on his person. But if he had been armed, and if Cole had just clammed up, the worst thing that could have happened last night was that von Phul could have shot Henwood.

And that would not have been weighing on Cole's conscience.

At times, he tried to focus on what could be considered a positive outcome. The very one that, admittedly, he felt guilty about, but both men were now out of his way. Henwood was in jail and von Phul was dead. Neither one of them would be an impediment to him being with Isabel. But every time he thought about it, he was further racked with guilt about his coveting another man's wife. And not only coveting her, not only committing adultery with her in his heart, but in the flesh, in her bed, and her bath tub.

The drive back to the ranch had been uncomfortable, to say the least. Not only was Springer there in the back seat with Isabel, but the mood was a difficult one to navigate. Besides Cole's conflicted feelings, there was also the shock that Isabel seemed to be experiencing, and the inscrutable reactions of Springer.

He may have been a shrewd businessman, but he seemed completely oblivious to his wife's indiscretions. It was a very quiet drive back.

It wasn't until a couple of days later that Cole had an opportunity to speak with Isabel. She was eating a solitary breakfast, and Cole was attending to her. Standing behind her, he watched her for a while, visually tracing the curve of her back as she sat slumped and despondent.

Finally, as she dabbed at her mouth and placed her napkin on the table, she took a deep breath and sighed, and she started to push her chair back. Cole rushed forward to help her, pulling the chair, and as she stood, he placed his hand gently on her shoulder.

Isabel started and looked at him, as if she had forgotten he was there.

"Isabel," he said quietly, realizing that now was not the time to use her nickname, "I'm here if you need me. If there's anything I can do to help you in this difficult time, please let me know."

"Yes, Cole," she replied, an expression of bewilderment on her face, "I certainly will. I must say, though, that this is highly inappropriate." She glanced at his hand resting on her shoulder.

"Of course, ma'am," he said, taking his hand away and looking toward the door, where someone could enter at any moment. "Please forgive me."

"We're all a bit flustered, now," Isabel said generously, sighing again as she walked toward the door.

Cole kicked himself for not using greater discretion. This was not the time. He busied himself at clearing her dishes.

§

The day was growing warm as the sun strolled across the sky. In the late morning, there was still a little shade on the west side of the windmill, and in its slight shelter, Cole stood there looking toward the mountains.

He ached for Isabel, to feel her body against him, to see her smile at him and kiss him again. But he understood the ordeal she was enduring now. He missed her, but he had to respect her needs, allow her to find her way back to him in her own time.

He missed Laura, too. He had written to her a few times, to tell her of his current situation. He had waxed poetic about the beauty of the country at the foot of the Rocky Mountains, and he described some of the details of his life here and his job. He left out details about Isabel. He wondered why Laura had never responded.

Laura had seemed sorry that he was leaving. The last time Cole saw her was the day before he left for Colorado. She had come over to say goodbye to him. She looked beautiful, dressed up in her Sunday best, as if she wanted his final memory to be of her looking her absolute finest. Cole couldn't imagine thinking about Laura any other way.

Cole's father was in his study working on his sermon for Sunday. His mother was in the kitchen preparing dinner. He didn't know where his brothers were, but Cole and Laura were somewhat alone. Cole had suggested they go for a walk in the woods that stood behind the garden.

It was a hot and humid day, and it felt good when they entered the shade of the trees. Laura had sighed as the shade washed over them, and she took Cole's hand, swinging it between them as he had seen sweethearts do.

"I'm going to miss you," he said.

"I wish you didn't have to go," she replied as she stopped and turned toward him.

"I know, sweetheart, I do too."

"You'll write to me?"

"Of course I will!" Laura smiled and leaned against him, placing her head on his chest. Cole put his arms around her, holding her close. The back of her dress was wet with sweat, but in the shade, it was cool. Cole thought that it was oddly tantalizing to feel her cool, wet dress, with the heat of her body coming through it.

"I think I've fallen in love with you," Laura said breathily. "I think I'll just die if I can't be with you."

She lifted her head and looked up at him, her mouth inches away from his. Impulsively, Cole pressed his lips against hers, and she responded immediately, pulling him closer. He felt that surge again when their lips parted and their tongues touched. Tasting her tongue and her lips aroused his appetite and made him want more.

When they parted, both panting for breath, Cole didn't want to let go of her, until Laura began unbuttoning his shirt. She pushed it back off his shoulders and stood there looking at him. Her eyes traveled down his chest, and he was sure she must have noticed the bulge in his trousers, but then she looked back up at his face.

For a moment, all Cole could do was look at her. He was enamored with her beautiful dark eyes, her dark hair, pulled back today into a ponytail, and as always, the freckles that disappeared down her chest. Laura allowed her arms to hang at her side, her shoulders back, her chest out, as if presenting herself to Cole.

"I wish I was dressed up for you," Cole said, appreciating how beautiful she looked.

"You look perfect," she replied, and all Cole could do was smile.

He started unbuttoning her dress, his breaths coming faster as he fumbled with the buttons between her breasts. Laura grinned and let him take as long as he needed. By the time her dress lay on the ground at her feet, Cole was, again, following the freckles down into her brassiere.

He could scarcely move, which was fine, because it was, apparently, Laura's turn again. She reached forward and unfastened Cole's jeans and pushed them down. She couldn't get them off, though, so Cole bent over and took his boots and socks off. While he was down there, he helped Laura out of her shoes, as well. Then, he stood back up and stepped out of his jeans.

As his hand slipped behind the waistband of Laura's petticoat to unfasten it, the feel of the soft skin of her lower back against his fingers caused him to shiver. His fingers were inches from her private parts, and suddenly, it was as if his fingers just wouldn't work properly.

Laura smiled at him again and decided it was time to help him out. She unfastened her petticoat, allowed it to drop down around her feet, and she pushed her pantalets down, and stepped out of them. Then, she came close to Cole, bringing her body against his to kiss him, and Cole put his arms around her. Her bare skin pressed against his was a feeling like nothing he had ever experienced, and in seconds, he was erect and hard.

Standing against him, Laura noticed at once. She pressed her body harder against him, and as she did this, Cole surprised himself by actually being able to get her brassiere unfastened while still engaged in kissing her. As she let it fall, she bent over and picked up their clothes, spreading them on the ground in front of a birch tree.

*She pushed her panties down, watching Cole's face the whole time. Cole didn't know what expression his face wore at the time, but she seemed pleased with his reaction. She was standing in front of him now, completely naked, and she was the most beautiful thing he had ever seen.*

*Laura pushed Cole's underwear down, then pulled him down onto their clothing, beside her. Kissing this beautiful, naked young woman, holding her body in his arms, was a most extraordinary sensation.*

*The most extraordinary sensation he had ever experienced, until a few weeks after he first met Isabel Springer.*

# 41

Isabel," Cole said after Isabel finished her breakfast a couple of days later, "is there anything at all that I can do for you?"

Before she had a chance to push her chair back and stand, Cole had knelt beside her and placed his arm around her shoulders, and he rested his other hand on her thigh, squeezing it affectionately. Isabel looked down at his hand on her leg.

"Cole, you must not do this!" she stated urgently. "This is not right!"

"I'm sorry, sweetheart, but it simply kills me to see you so unhappy."

The stress of her current situation was obviously weighing on her. Her eyes filled with tears as she looked at Cole, but she mustered a serious tone of voice when she replied.

"My happiness, or lack thereof, is none of your concern."

"You're wrong, my dear. Your happiness means everything to me." Cole was worried that, in the time that had elapsed since their lovemaking, one of his competitors might have won Isabel's affection away from him. He decided to remind her. "And I know you care about me, too. You said so that first night in your bedroom."

"Is this yet another paramour of yours?" Springer said sternly from the door.

Cole had not heard him enter, and he removed his arm from Isabel's shoulders, quickly standing at attention. Springer was finally made aware of Isabel's chronic unfaithfulness when her letters were found among von Phul's personal effects the day he died.

"John," Isabel exclaimed as she stood up herself, her voice taut.

"My wife may not be the picture of fidelity, young man, but she's still my wife, at least until the divorce is granted. I do not approve of her whoring around under my roof, whether it's with a friend or with a member of my staff."

"John, this is not what –"

"I've not yet decided what to do about the friend," Springer continued, ignoring Isabel's protest, "but it's clear what must be done about the employee." He looked severely at Cole. "You will gather up your things and you will leave this house."

"Sir, I'm –"

"At once!" Springer emphasized, raising his voice and emphasizing each syllable.

Cole looked at Isabel, wondering if she would stick up for him. She seemed intimidated by Springer's anger and stood there silently, but then Cole had a fleeting thought that, given the fact that Springer was divorcing Isabel, she might choose to leave with him. But she just stood there, her eyes down. He looked back at Springer, who was watching him intently.

"Yes sir," Cole finally said quietly.

§

Rupert Coleman looked at his nephew, not sure what to say. Cole had gone to the bunkhouse with his suitcase, and as he told his uncle about his indiscretions with Isabel, cringing with embarrassment, Uncle Rupert had listened to his story, his mouth hanging open.

Several times, the bunkhouse started burning, flames climbing and blackening the walls, but Cole managed to hold it together until he completed his story. The smell of sulfur was strong in his nose.

"Boy," Uncle Rupert finally said, "didn't I warn you about that?"

"Yes, Uncle Rupert, you did," Cole nodded. The nod turned into a back and forth shake as he acknowledged his imprudence. "I know, I was stupid."

Uncle Rupert looked at him, shaking his head.

"So, where do you think you'll go?" he asked.

"I'll probably go back home," Cole sighed. "Maybe Laura will still have me."

"Laura? Laura Franklin?"

"Yes, you remember her?"

"I do." Uncle Rupert looked at Cole with an inscrutable look on his face.

"We were in love before I came out here. I just hope I haven't messed that up."

"You think Laura Franklin was in love with you?" Cole didn't understand his uncle's disbelieving tone.

"Cole," Uncle Rupert said hesitantly, "Laura Franklin wasn't in love with you. She was afraid of you."

"What?" Cole scoffed. "No, you must be thinking of someone else. Laura was this pretty girl back home. We saw each other all the time. We were in love."

"No, Cole, Laura –"

"Dammit, Uncle Rupert!" Cole exclaimed, then he stopped and took a deep breath. "Sorry," he said, "but we –" He flinched for a moment, but, having been so frank with his uncle about his time with Isabel, he felt emboldened to reveal more about his relationship with Laura. "Laura and I, well, we had relations the day before I left for Colorado."

"No, son," Uncle Rupert replied quietly, sadly, "you didn't."

Cole peered at his uncle as his vision turned dark and red, the flames finally starting to take hold.

"Don't you remember, boy?" Uncle Rupert continued. "She complained to your father about you."

Cole struggled as the bunkhouse began shuddering violently, the flames climbing the walls.

# 42

It was early when Suzy arrived at the Spotswood Institute. She knew Fin was interested in finishing Cole's story before sending him on to the next place. However, she was uneasy about the effect it was having on him. The hallucinations related to the medication Fin had been taking, since they usually happened during the night or early morning, were leaving him exhausted. Combine that with Cole's episodes and *his* hallucinations, and Fin was in bad shape.

She hoped that if Fin insisted on finishing Cole's story, she could at least support him through it, and then quickly send Cole away.

Her hopes were dashed when she arrived.

There was a lot of activity around Fin's room. The door was standing open, and doctors, nurses and assistants were rushing in and out. When she got to the door, she saw a couple of people bent over Fin, examining him. He seemed unconscious. Dr. Ivanov was standing just inside the door.

"Dr. Ivanov," she said, feeling the panic beginning. "What's wrong with Fin?"

"Ah, Ms. Queenn," he replied, smiling, oddly enough. He took her arm and smoothly guided her outside the room. "Nurse discovered Feen this morning apparently awake but unresponsive."

"Apparently awake?" Suzy echoed, glancing back toward Fin's room.

"Heart rate, pulse, respiration are consistent with awake, but Feen does not respond to outside stimuli."

"Do you have any idea what's causing this condition?"

"At moment, no," he smiled again, probably thinking it would have a calming effect. "But we are looking into it and will let you know."

Suzy noticed that he had guided her toward the waiting area and, with that dismissal, was turning to go back now. She took a deep breath.

"Doctor?" Doctor Ivanov stopped and looked at her. Suzy closed her eyes and blew out the breath, hoping she was doing the right thing. "I think I know what it is."

Dr. Ivanov turned and looked at her curiously. Suzy hesitated until he began looking impatient.

"I am what some might call a spirit medium." Dr. Ivanov frowned, confused. "I can communicate with spirits of the dead. Recently, Fin has been developing that ability as well." The skepticism showing on Dr. Ivanov's face was not surprising. "Are you aware that there's a ghost in this building?"

"I am sorry, Ms. Queenn," he replied, shaking his head, "I really must get back to my patient's room."

"Dr. Ivanov," Suzy said with a little more force than she had planned, "are you aware –"

"I have heard silly stories," he interrupted, exasperated, "but I do not have time for them now."

"If you want to help Fin, you'll take a couple of minutes to hear me out."

Dr. Ivanov glanced back toward Fin's room, then sighed and turned back to Suzy, crossing his arms in front of him.

"This place," she began, "started out as an insane asylum back in 1900."

"I am aware of history of building," Dr. Ivanov replied with some irritation. Resisting the urge to tell him to shut the hell up and listen, Suzy continued.

"One of the patients was a man named Arthur Coleman, who was subject to severe hallucinations. We've been learning his story over the last couple of days, and I think Fin may have continued without me this morning.

"But I'm afraid Cole's hallucinations have been affecting Fin pretty severely, for a couple of reasons. First, the hallucinations themselves are frightening and they stay with him. But also, the fact that Fin himself has been having hallucinations of his own, and because they both come from a strict religious background, Fin identifies with Cole.

185

"Some of Cole's hallucinations have been of a religious nature, and that has triggered Fin's own guilt in relation to his religious past."

"Ms. Queenn," Dr. Ivanov sighed, giving in to his impatience, "I do not see what your story has to do with Feen's condition."

"This is the condition we both go into when connecting with ghosts," she gestured toward Fin's room. "It's almost like an out-of-body experience."

Dr. Ivanov narrowed his eyes at Suzy. He shook his head and put his hands up, and Suzy knew he was about to dismiss her.

"Is he in any danger?" Suzy asked quickly.

"Een danger?"

"If you don't wake him up right now, will it hurt him in any way?"

"Probably not, but since we don't know what ees cause of condition, we are concerned."

"Well, I'm concerned, too, but I just told you the cause of it," Suzy said, her own irritation seeping into her voice. "So, if there's no danger to Fin, can you just put a hold on trying to revive him? I don't know for certain, but trying to sever his connection to Cole by force could be even more damaging to him. Let me have a couple of hours." She couldn't tell if his stance was softening or not. "Please, let me try."

Dr. Ivanov looked at her sternly for a few moments. Finally, he shook his head again and sighed.

"Alright, we will wait. I will give you hour."

"Doctor, a couple of hours, please." Dr. Ivanov resisted, but Suzy persisted. "If, during that time," she conceded, "he goes into arrest or displays any other signs of trauma, you can intervene, but please, let me try to get Cole to break the connection."

"*Súka!*" Dr. Ivanov exclaimed. "Fine, two hours."

"Thank you, Doctor!" Suzy replied. She didn't know if she could accomplish her goal in that time. She was in new

186

territory, but she got what she had asked for. She hoped it would be enough.

She followed Dr. Ivanov as he turned and went back into Fin's room, still shaking his head. There were two people in the room, Peter and a nurse Suzy hadn't met before. Peter had the electronic tablet from Fin's doorway in his hand, scrolling through his record, or possibly the internet, looking for answers about Fin's condition. The nurse was taking Fin's pulse.

"We will stop for now," Dr. Ivanov announced. Peter and the nurse looked up at him. He motioned toward the door. "Ms. Queenn thinks Feen ees connected to ghost." His tone was contemptuous. "Since there ees no immediate danger to patient, I have agreed to allow her time to prove silly theory."

Peter and the nurse glanced at each other, then gathered up the things they had brought into the room. Dr. Ivanov looked up at Suzy with his best stern expression.

"We will continue monitoring Feen's condition." Fin's monitor had been removed a couple of days before, but Suzy saw that it was back, with wires snaking across the bed to his hand, chest and head. "I will let you have two hours for ghost communication," he shook his head again and rolled his eyes, "but eef condition worsens, we will take over."

"Thank you, Doctor," Suzy replied. "I appreciate it."

Dr. Ivanov turned and left, making a point of leaving the door open.

## 43

Y our father wrote to me about Laura Franklin just before he sent you out here," Uncle Rupert explained. "She wasn't a girl as you seem to remember. She was a woman in her thirties."

Cole struggled with the memory. Uncle Rupert must be mistaken. Cole remembered Laura vividly. He remembered her voice. He remembered her beautiful dark hair and eyes. He remembered her body, the freckles that traveled down her neck and chest.

No, Uncle Rupert was wrong. He was obviously thinking about someone else. Cole noticed his uncle's features were looking distorted to him, but he tried to ignore it.

"She was a woman in your father's church. She had left her abusive husband, and your father agreed to allow her to stay with your family. That's when he made that unused shed out back into living quarters, and Laura moved in there, in exchange for helping out around your father's little farm."

Cole recalled the shed behind his parents' home, next to the garden. He had seen it a few months ago, and several times since, when he recalled that time when Laura helped him pick corn, then sat with him against the shed. That's when she took off her shirt and brassiere in front of him.

Except that what he was seeing now was different. He saw the shed, and the eight foot tall buttonbush that grew next to it, on the back side, away from his house. His mother had often stated her desire to trim the bush, as it was growing like a weed. She didn't want it to take over the yard. Cole was fine with it as it was. He saw the foliage that darkened the window on that side of the shed.

Cole was standing, now, between the buttonbush and the shed, hidden by the dense foliage. Not only was he hidden from anybody on the outside, but also from Laura, as long as she didn't come close to the window and try to look through it. And she never did, since the view was completely blocked by the bush.

Cole was sweaty from his time picking corn with Laura, but when he suggested that they sit in the shade of the shed, Laura had declined and went inside. That's when Cole took his position in the buttonbush.

*And his action paid off. There was Laura, in the supposed privacy of her little home, peeling off her sweaty shirt and brassiere. She really was a lovely woman, her dark exotic beauty tempered by the innocence of those fascinating freckles that, as he saw now, and many times since, traveled down her chest, across her breasts and onto her belly.*

*Cole watched as she poured water into her wash basin. The shed didn't have plumbing, but Laura never complained. He watched as she wet a washcloth and began washing herself.*

*That was when he fell in love with Laura, and when his visions of hellfire began.*

§

*"You're right, Uncle Rupert," Cole said, "she was older than I remembered." He frowned, struggling to hold on to his memories. "But still, we were in love. The day before I came out here, we were walking in the woods, and she told me she loved me. She said she'd die if she couldn't be with me."*

*"Cole," Uncle Rupert said cautiously, "do you really think that sounds like something a woman in her thirties would say to a boy?"*

*Cole squeezed his eyes shut tight when horns grew out of Uncle Rupert's head. Cole clearly remembered Laura going with him into the woods that day.*

*Only she didn't. He saw her now in the home she had made in their shed, from the vantage point of the buttonbush. After she had talked to his father.*

*She had complained to him about Cole following her around. She said he was bothering her. It was as if she had forgotten how much Cole loved her. He thought he had made it clear, but obviously, he had to try harder to make her see.*

*He peered through the window, safe in the dense shade of the tall bush. Most of the time, when he watched Laura through the window, she was fully clothed. But even then, it was still thrilling to watch her. Sharing the intimacy of her private life with him only made him love her more.*

*But it was especially wonderful when she shared her body with him, too. As she did now. It looked like she was planning on going*

189

somewhere. She took off all of her clothes and washed her body thoroughly, then dried off. She put on clean clothes, including bloomers and a petticoat, under a pretty dress.

No, she wasn't going somewhere. She was getting dressed up for Cole!

Thinking about Laura taking this extra step, getting dressed up in her Sunday clothes for him, made his heart fill to overflowing with love for her. And it made him forgive her for complaining to his father about him just a couple of hours earlier.

Then, he realized that Laura wasn't the problem. His father must have misunderstood her. That had to be it. Cole knew that a woman who would go to this much trouble to look this good for him would not be afraid of him.

He remembered the talk his father had with him, warning him to stay away from Laura, to stop following her around. His words were practically incomprehensible. The thoughts he expressed had no relation to real life.

His *real life*, with Laura.

*Sweet Jesus, she was a lovely woman!* He needed to go in there. He needed to acknowledge her efforts to look her best for him. It was important to let a woman know that she was appreciated.

He pulled himself out of the buttonbush and walked around the back of the shed. He had been inside her little home many times, when she wasn't there. It was a shed. His father had never installed a lock on the door, but it was understood that it was Laura's home and that they were not to enter. That rule, though, could not be imposed upon her greatest love. Cole knew that Laura would welcome him with her. His father was so strict, she probably just didn't want him to know about their love.

Cole didn't either. Not yet. As he came around the back side of the shed, he peeked around the corner toward the house and didn't see any movement in any of the windows. Fortunately, the rooms that were most often occupied were at the front of the house.

He approached the door to the shed and paused. He took a deep breath and smoothed his hair back. He wished that he was dressed up, as well, but he couldn't take the time for that now. He turned the knob and went inside, pushing the door closed behind him.

Laura looked up at the sound of the door, and she gasped. God, she was beautiful! Even now, seeing Cole, her eyes went wide, and her jaw dropped as she was pleasantly surprised to see him there with her.

Cole knew, though, that she might inadvertently make too much noise and unwittingly alert his parents to their clandestine meeting, so he rushed to her, wrapping his arms around her, pressing his lips to hers.

Laura was overcome by his ardor, and she struggled in her passion to push him away. Cole realized that he wasn't giving her the opportunity to breathe, so he pulled away from her, but only long enough to allow her to take a breath. Then, his lips were pressed tightly against hers again, his tongue probing against them.

In the excitement of the moment, Laura brought her knee up, and it made contact with his testicles. Cole doubled over in pain, and Laura pushed herself away from him. As she was bent backwards in his arm, though, she was off balance, her heel broke, and she fell over, falling upon the brick hearth under the little wood stove that heated the shed in the winter.

Cole took deep breaths, his hands gently holding his stones. He was confused for a moment. Laura was so still. Was she waiting for him to come down there to her? The pain was subsiding now. He knew that had been an accident. He needed to show her that he held no ill feelings about it.

He got down on his knees next to her, looking into her eyes. It was strange, though. Her eyes weren't focused on him. It was as if she was looking at something behind him, even though he was right in front of her.

He cradled her head in his hand, and that's when he felt the warm sticky ooze on the back of her head, against the bricks. Something told him he needed to leave.

One last look, one last kiss, and he left the shed.

§

"The heel of her shoe had broken," Uncle Rupert said, watching Cole closely, "and, apparently, she tripped. Laura's dead, Cole."

"I remember," Cole said slowly. The moments after that had been a blur, until now.

He had left the shed and fled into the woods behind the garden. Even then, with Laura gone, she wasn't really. He could feel her with him. They walked together, holding hands until she stopped him and began undressing for him.

The memory of reclining there on the ground beneath the tree still made him hard, so he tried to rein in the memory while he was there with Uncle Rupert. He just couldn't, though.

Holding Laura in his arms, caressing her naked body, kissing her lips – that afternoon was still one of his favorite memories. Feeling her smooth skin, her soft breast under his hand, and that wonderful black tangle of hair between her legs.

If only they hadn't been interrupted! Laura had fled when she heard his mother come looking for him. Unfortunately, though, Cole hadn't heard her.

"Oh, my dear Lord!" his mother exclaimed when she saw Cole there under the tree, naked. She quickly turned away, hiding her eyes. Laura had been kissing him, straddling his privy member, until his mother showed up. Then, she left Cole holding it in his hand.

When the situation finally penetrated Cole's mind, he quickly pulled his clothes over him, wondering how Laura had gotten her clothes out from under him.

Cole remembered now that his mother hadn't been there at the station to say goodbye to him the next morning.

His thoughts alternated now, between Isabel and Laura, their faces, their features, their bodies transposable in his mind.

He missed her desperately.

He wondered if she still loved him.

He didn't know which one he was wondering that about.

## 44

Suzy came out of the episode, feeling the usual temporary fatigue and disorientation. Along with a new feeling of creepiness about Cole.

She took a deep breath and sighed heavily, looking up toward Fin's bed. He was still unconscious. Suzy frowned, knowing he should have emerged from it at the same time. Had another episode started and Suzy had, somehow, avoided it?

She stood up from her chair and sat down on the edge of the bed, taking Fin's hand in hers.

"Fin," she said softly, "Fin, please come back."

But he just lay there, breathing softly, oblivious to the world, and to Suzy's presence. Suzy's apprehension began growing, and she struggled to keep the panic at bay.

She saw a movement in her peripheral vision, and she glanced toward the door. Dr. Ivanov was standing there watching her. She turned back toward Fin, choosing to ignore the doctor's apparent judgment.

She decided she needed to do some meditation. The floor was covered with hard tile, so she moved back to her chair, making herself as comfortable as possible. She needed to relax, to open her mind and heart.

She needed to make contact with Cole.

# 45

He hadn't been careful enough. It was little wonder Cole was in this situation now.

Isabel had not stuck up for him against Springer, but just stood there mute. That had been a blow. Then, while he was in the bunkhouse with Uncle Rupert, Jimmy and Buck, a couple of the other ranch hands, came in and were talking about those damn letters that Isabel had written to von Phul. They had just been made public, and now Isabel was fleeing to Chicago to escape the shame.

His own shame and guilt had resurfaced as Cole had revealed the nature of his relationship with Isabel to Uncle Rupert, and then that conversation brought back the shame and guilt of his relationship with Laura. In lucid moments, he remembered Laura dying, and the part he played in that event.

Even though nobody suspected him of that, nor of his illicit relationship with her, he knew that God would hold him responsible. God knew about all of it. Cole's judgment day was not going to be a pleasant one.

The present day was not looking very sunny, either.

The realizations about Laura and Isabel all coming down on him at once caused his visions of hell to intensify.

"What's wrong with you, boy?" Uncle Rupert asked.

Cole didn't realize that he was rocking back and forth with his eyes squeezed shut. It took a few moments for him to notice that Uncle Rupert had spoken. He could barely hear his voice over the popping and crackling of the fire, and the screams of other unseen unfortunates like himself.

"Come on, son, I need to get back to work." Uncle Rupert spoke with the voice of someone who didn't know how to react to someone else's bizarre behavior. A little annoyance, a little impatience, possibly even a little fear.

Cole opened his eyes and looked at his uncle. His lower eyelids were drooping down his cheeks, his skin sliding down his face as if it were melting in the heat of the flames. As Cole watched, Uncle Rupert's eyeballs bulged and suddenly popped.

Cole jumped, digging his fingers into the edge of the bed. He wasn't aware that he was screaming until Jimmy and Buck rushed back in. Uncle Rupert was already holding on to Cole, trying to calm him down, but Cole was fighting him, his eyes like saucers as he looked at the melted, mangled face dripping off of the skull in front of him.

Seeing no other option, Buck grabbed a rope and tied Cole's hands and feet.

§

The Arapahoe County Asylum for the Mentally Ill was a big, impressive, and very modern, brick building. Built just eleven years before, it was the latest in the care and seclusion of the insane, which Uncle Rupert was now convinced that Cole was.

"Uncle Rupert," Cole pleaded, "please don't do this! I'll do better." Struggling and crying, they had actually had to tie him to the seat of the wagon.

"I'm sorry, son," Uncle Rupert said as he stopped the wagon in front of the building. "Screaming and raving about hellfire raging in the bunkhouse, and about my face melting in the heat, and this in front of the other ranch hands." He leaned on his knees and looked sympathetically at Cole. "You can't stay at the ranch, now that Springer's let you go. I wouldn't feel right just sending you somewhere else to be someone else's problem, like my brother did. I'm afraid this is not something we can hide any longer. It's a real problem that needs to be dealt with."

Two orderlies dressed in white came out the front door, having been called ahead of time. They wordlessly helped Uncle Rupert untie Cole and get him down off the wagon. Each of the men taking an arm, they led Cole up to the front door, as Uncle Rupert followed. Cole's struggles had little effect on the men.

They were greeted inside the door by a man in a white coat.

"I'm Doctor Mead," he said, shaking Uncle Rupert's hand, and basically ignoring Cole.

"Hello, Doctor," Uncle Rupert replied. "Thank you for meeting us."

"Of course, it's my pleasure. That's what we're here for." He now turned his attention to Cole. "And this is Arthur?"

"Yes, sir," Uncle Rupert said quietly, his eyes turned downward as if he was ashamed. Cole didn't know if he was ashamed of what he was doing, or if he was ashamed of Cole.

"Tom and Randall will get Cole settled," Dr. Mead said, nodding to the two men. "Come with me and we'll take care of the paperwork."

Cole watched as Uncle Rupert followed the doctor into an office on the right, until Tom and Randall turned him around and led him to a doorway. The shorter one, Tom, pushed a key into the lock and turned it, opening the door and leading Cole into a long hallway. He couldn't tell if what he was seeing was another hallucination of hell, or if it was real.

The hallway was dark, with a few scattered bare electric bulbs hanging from the ceiling. Both walls were lined with heavy doors with small barred windows. A few of the doors were open, but most were closed, and a few of those had the hands of the occupants sticking out, the fingers extended in a pleading, imploring gesture.

From a distant room, he heard somebody screaming repeatedly. Closer to this end, in a cell on the right, he heard someone talking in a normal voice. Then, the same voice responded.

Just ahead, from a door on the left, he heard a deep, mournful voice coming through the barred window.

"Oh, lonely death on lonely life! Oh, now I feel my topmost greatness lies in my topmost grief. Ho, ho! from all your furthest bounds, pour ye now in, ye bold billows of my whole foregone life, and top this one piled comber of my death!" As they came alongside the door, Cole could hear the voice more clearly, and it was then that he recognized the words. One of the inmates was reading from or reciting Moby Dick. "Towards thee I roll, thou all-destroying but unconquering whale; to the last I grapple with thee; from hell's heart I stab at thee; for hate's sake I spit my last breath at thee. Sink all coffins and all hearses to one common pool! and since neither can be mine, let me then tow to pieces, while still chasing thee, though tied to thee, thou damned whale! Thus, I give up the spear!"

"Captain Ahab's at it again," Randal sneered. Tom snickered in response.

*They stopped in front of a set of double doors, and Cole felt his heart lurch, wondering what was on the other side. Tom knocked on the door, and it was unlocked and opened from inside by another orderly, employed, apparently, as a guard. He was a disagreeable-looking man, about fifty pounds overweight, all of it hanging around his gut. His face had a built-in scowl, his forehead permanently creased with a vertical slash between his eyebrows.*

*"We got somebody new for you," said Randall as he pushed Cole unceremoniously through the door. "This is Arthur."*

*"Cole," Cole corrected.*

*"I beg your pardon?" Randall asked.*

*"My name is Arthur Coleman. People call me Cole."*

*"Cole, Arthur, whatever," Tom replied. "I don't care what you call me, just don't call me late for dinner." The other two men seemed to think that was pretty funny.*

*"I do care what you call me, though, bonehead," the guard said to Cole. "I'm Mr. Sawyer. Call me that, or sir." Cole was distracted by his new surroundings and was surprised when Sawyer poked him in the chest. "Did you hear me, boy?"*

*"Yes, sir."*

*"Alright, that's better. Keep that in mind, and we shouldn't have any problems."*

*Cole wasn't really paying attention to him anymore. He was looking around the room that he had been brought into. It was a large room with high windows on the wall on his left. There were benches arranged against the walls around the perimeter, and a few tables and chairs scattered about in the middle of the room.*

*The people in the 'activities room' as Sawyer referred to it, brought a tear to Cole's eye and a lump to his throat. They were dressed in loose-fitting clothing, some little more than a long lightweight shirt. Some of them were rocking back and forth, their eyes vacant. A couple of them were moving their hands as if gesturing, but they weren't talking. A few of them were actually talking to each other, but for the most part, the people in the room seemed to be in a world of their own.*

*"Anything I should know about him?" Sawyer asked Cole's two escorts.*

"He doesn't seem to be violent," Randall said, shaking his head. "But he hasn't been here long. Just keep an eye on him. His uncle's in the process of admitting him now."

Sawyer nodded and took Cole's shoulder, grasping it a little tighter than Cole thought was necessary, and pushed him into the room.

As Cole looked around, the flames started climbing the walls, turning some of the poor inmates into smoldering lumps of ash. He looked up and saw the large face of an old and apparently angry man, with white hair and a beard, watching him from near the ceiling, through the blinding smoke. The man opened his mouth and addressed Cole with a deep and resonant voice that shook the room, though nobody else seemed to notice.

"Arthur Coleman," he thundered, "thou hast been found guilty of sins of the flesh and of the heart. Thou art wicked and unrepentant. I cast thee into the lake which burneth with fire and brimstone, to be tormented forever and ever."

Well, Cole thought, squaring his shoulders, it came a little earlier than I expected, but it's time to face the music.

ole." The voice echoed in his consciousness, but not like the voice of God. This was a feminine voice, soft and mellow, but he thought he sensed a little tension, as well.

She was sitting there in her chair, beside Fin's bed. He knew she couldn't see him, unless he wanted her to. She sure was a pretty thing. He decided to just look at her for a while.

"Cole," she said again, in her mind, "Cole, please talk to me."

He couldn't resist her pleading tone.

"I'm here," he said, and suddenly, she could see him.

"Oh, thank you, Cole. Thank you for speaking to me. And thank you for sharing your life with us."

Cole frowned as he looked at her. His view of her quivered, and he struggled to hold it still, and to keep the flames away.

"You can still thank me after what you know?"

"You've had a difficult time," Suzy said, "with your illness and the guilt that you feel, and being placed here." She shook her head. "I probably wouldn't handle all of that very well either."

Cole felt the sensation of a lump in his throat and tears filling his eyes, even though he knew he no longer had an actual throat or eyes.

"I couldn't help it," he said as the tears tumbled down his cheeks.

"I know," Suzy said sympathetically. "It's okay. It was all a long time ago." Suzy realized too late that Cole might not be aware of how much time had passed, or even that he was dead. He screwed up his face at her comment, but Suzy forged ahead before he had a chance to ask about it. "Cole, I need to ask you about Fin."

Cole looked at Fin lying there in his bed.

"What about him?"

"Are you – are you holding on to him somehow? He's not waking up."

"I don't . . . think so." Cole frowned as he looked at Fin and back at Suzy.

"Cole," Suzy said, her expression becoming serious, "you need to move on."

"Move on?"

"To the next place."

"What do you mean?"

"As I understand it, there's something like a door there where you are, with a light on the other side. You need to go through that door."

Cole began shaking, overcome by fear, and he couldn't hold back the inferno. Everything around him erupted in flames.

"I can't do that," he said as tears filled his eyes.

"Yes, you can, Cole," Suzy said, trying to keep her voice level and calm.

Cole pictured the *real* flames of hell that he would suffer if he went through that door and met God face-to-face. The thought of that eternal torment terrified him, and he violently shook his head back and forth.

"No!" he shouted, as his body was suddenly engulfed in the blazes of hell. Then, he disappeared from Suzy's sight.

§

Suzy couldn't let Cole go. She had to hold on to her connection with him somehow. She concentrated on remaining relaxed and focused, but emotionally, she felt abraded and raw.

She remembered the moments after Mark and Emma went over the edge of their boat three years ago. Suzy had been driving, and struck a glancing blow off an overturned boat, and then another, harder blow off a nearby rock. Turning back, she remembered the feeling of panic in her chest as she looked in vain for them, but knew they were gone.

That feeling was threatening to return as she thought that she might be losing Fin. She was finding it difficult to breathe, as if her chest was constricted. She had no idea what would happen if Cole stayed here, if he kept whatever hold he had on Fin. But Fin's continued coma-like state gave her a pretty good idea.

Suzy wasn't aware of the tears slipping down her cheeks as she pushed that thought from her mind, concentrating on her connection with Cole.

She couldn't lose Fin, too.

§

Cole walked around aimlessly, his thoughts a jumble. He usually stayed in the vicinity of the room that had been his, but with the disturbing thoughts that Suzy had introduced, he was just wandering. Still, he tried to stay alert.

He glanced over his shoulder and saw the outline, the "door" that Suzy had referred to. The outline was white, from the bright light that always seemed to seep through around the edges from the other side. He remembered when he had first seen the light, unobstructed by the door.

Years ago, influenza had swept through the asylum, and several patients and even a few of the staff succumbed to its effects. Cole had been one of the first to go.

He had been lying in the infirmary, covered by several blankets, but they weren't enough to stem the chills. The coughing was relentless. The day before, he had started coughing up blood. Finally, he drifted off to welcome sleep, but he opened his eyes again almost immediately.

That's when he saw the light, the door standing wide open near his bed, the bright whiteness pouring through. He had gotten up from the bed to investigate, marveling that he actually had the strength to get up. But he couldn't see anything through the portal, just the blinding white light.

As he hesitated there, the door eventually closed, but the light still shone around the edges. He looked up and down the rows of beds, at the nurses, and the doctor, tending to other patients, and he thought it strange that nobody else seemed to notice the dazzling light that had flooded into the infirmary moments before.

Shaking his head in wonder, he turned around. That's when he saw his body, still on the bed, still covered up with blankets, and no longer breathing. He had stood there staring at himself for what seemed like a long time although, admittedly, time seemed to have taken on a dreamlike state. It was difficult to tell how much had passed.

Cole had a hard time determining what he thought about seeing his dead body lying there, alone and, as yet, undiscovered by the medical staff. He had spent his whole life afraid of death and, especially, the judgment that he knew was waiting.

Death had released him from his physical afflictions, and it might have released him from his gloomy and miserable existence in the Arapahoe County Asylum for the Mentally Ill if not for his fear of the light coming through that door. Cole had always thought that if anyone wasn't truly mentally ill when they entered, and he was certain there were some, they surely were by the time they had been there a few years.

There had been some who had progressed in their treatment to the point of being released, but Cole never saw that outcome for himself. Death had been his release, although he certainly didn't expect hell to be a welcome replacement. His wraithlike existence in the asylum wasn't much better.

He turned and looked again at the door. It wasn't actually a door like the ones he was familiar with. There were no hinges, no doorknob. In fact, he couldn't really tell what the mechanism was. There was just the outline of white light showing him where it was located.

He stepped warily toward it, and as he approached, the portal opened again, pouring its blazing white light into the infirmary, where only he could see it. He stopped, certain that if he went through it, God would be waiting there to cast him into the lake of fire.

He decided right then that he would not go through it. The option was always there. Every time he came near it, it opened, so he knew that if he ever decided in the future to face up to his sins, it would be there. But not now.

The part that was particularly disconcerting to him was the fact that the crazy thing followed him around. Wherever he went, he could look over his shoulder, and it would be there. And it was seldom placed in a wall, like a real door would be. It was usually hanging against nothing, with whatever room or hallway he was in showing around it and through it.

At least until it opened, at which time the room showing through the door disappeared and only the white light was visible through the opening.

And now, this Suzy person had told him that he had to go through that door. Cole realized that he had been displaying a certain amount of arrogance in thinking that he could avoid punishment for his sins. "Be not deceived; God is not mocked: for whatsoever a man soweth, that shall he also reap." Still, to voluntarily go through that portal and meet his Maker, knowing what awaited him – no, he couldn't do that.

He realized that he was back at the door to his cell, and he stopped, knowing that Suzy and Fin were in there now. He didn't know if he was ready to face them. Suzy, especially. He had never come across anyone who could actually make contact with him, and would do so intentionally. She was formidable.

And to his immediate consternation, she appeared directly in front of him now.

## 47

Suzy was probably as surprised as Cole seemed to be when she found herself in front of him, in his world. She assumed this was what she had heard called by various names, the 'other side,' the astral plane, or a dimension of existence populated by spirit beings before birth or after death. She was shocked that she had somehow managed to cross over into it, since she was in neither state. But she had heard stories about those who had managed such an achievement, a so-called "out-of-body experience."

Her need, her intensity must have had something to do with it. But despite the urgency she felt, she couldn't help glancing at her surroundings. The carpeted hallway of the sleek Spotswood Institute was gone. In its place was a dingy hall lit by dim, sporadically-placed old-fashioned light bulbs. The entrances into the rooms, no longer sporting electronic tablets mounted in their holders, were now heavy metal doors, each with a small barred window.

She shuddered when she realized that this was what Cole saw every day from the time he had been admitted until he died, and every day since.

"What –!" Cole looked at Suzy, startled. "What are you doing here?"

Suzy saw the white outline behind Cole, and she immediately recognized what it was.

"You need to go through that door, Cole," Suzy replied, forcefully.

"I can't do that!" Suzy noticed that, despite the intensity of his response, he kept his voice down.

"You have some kind of hold on Fin," Suzy said imploringly. "He can't wake up. He's in something like a coma."

Cole scrunched his eyebrows together as he thought about what she said.

"I'm sorry," he said. "I don't mean to hurt anybody. But I can't go through that door."

"Why not?" Suzy asked, raising her voice in impatience.

With an anxious look on his face, Cole moved toward Suzy and pushed her toward the hard metal door of the cell behind her. Suzy braced herself for the impact, but to her surprise, they slipped through the door, into the dingy cell.

Looking around, she saw that the renovation of the Spotswood Institute didn't follow the exact floorplan of the asylum. Cole's old cell was tiny, much smaller than Fin's current room, and the furnishings were sparse. There was a cot, a small nightstand with a couple of books on it, and that seemed to be it.

Suzy's heart went out to Cole, but she was determined to not lose sight of why she was here. She looked back at Cole, and she was surprised to see the white outline behind him. It had followed him into the cell.

"I've done bad things," Cole said. "You know that. You've seen my life. You know why I can't go through that door."

"What do you think is on the other side?"

"God is there. Judgment. Punishment for my numerous sins."

"Cole," Suzy said, but then she stopped, taking a breath as she looked at him for a few moments before she continued. "Okay, it's not my place to try to change your belief system. If you believe God is there waiting to punish you after all these years, who am I to say you're wrong? But if you also believe that God is all-knowing and all-powerful, if he really wanted to punish you, do you really think his plans would be hindered by something so simple as you not wanting to go through a door?" She looked at him, peering into his eyes. "Besides, I assume you believe that God is merciful and loving."

Cole looked at her, his forehead wrinkled in thought, as a scripture came to mind.

"The Lord God, merciful and gracious, longsuffering, and abundant in goodness and truth."

"There you go!" Suzy said enthusiastically, seizing onto that verse and requoting it back to him excitedly. "God is merciful and gracious!" She noticed that Cole looked around nervously.

"'Forgiving iniquity and transgression and sin,'" he continued quoting, "'and that will by no means clear the guilty.' I'm guilty, Suzy. I'm a sinner, and I deserve to be punished. But I'm too much of a coward to go and receive it."

"You're not a coward," Suzy shook her head. "If God really was as rigid and harsh as that, I'd be afraid, too. But the verse you just quoted said that God's merciful and gracious, he forgives sin."

Cole's face puckered a little, looking almost like a little boy who was about to cry.

"But I've committed so many of them," he said. "How can he forgive me of all those?"

"I know you're sorry about them," Suzy said. "When we were watching your life, I saw what you saw. I felt your feelings, thought your thoughts."

"I thought those thoughts all the time!" Cole insisted. "I'm a repeat offender."

Suzy sighed. She wasn't a religious person, and she found it tiring to be arguing religion with someone who *was* religious. Suddenly, she remembered a fragment of a verse from one of the times she attended church with her parents when she was young.

"'If you should mark iniquities, O Lord, who could stand?' He punishes sinners if they're unrepentant. Nobody's perfect. Does he punish everybody for every mistake they make?" Cole looked at her for a moment, taken aback by her question. She didn't wait for him to answer. "What's the point of confession or penitence if we're just going to be punished anyway?"

Cole pondered her argument for a few moments.

"I suppose that makes sense," he said. "But how can you be sure?"

"I'm *not* sure," Suzy admitted. She didn't want to reveal that she was a heathen and possibly have Cole refuse her suggestion to leave. "The fact is none of us can be absolutely certain until we get there. But as you said, it makes sense. Based on your belief system, it's logical." She sighed. "You're a decent person, Cole. You've just had some tough circumstances to deal with. And if I can see that, certainly God can."

Suzy could tell that Cole was honestly thinking about it, and she was encouraged that he wasn't rejecting it outright.

"And I think you might make a few more points with God," she continued, "by letting Fin go."

Cole looked up at her, then he looked over to the side, where the wall of his cell was. Suzy followed his gaze and she gasped as she saw Fin lying in his hospital bed. She could now see the modern room in the Spotswood Institute, which was larger than Cole's little cell.

And there, to the side of his bed, she saw herself sitting in the chair, apparently unconscious. It was strange, scary, looking at herself as a separate entity, a disembodied consciousness viewing her extraneous physical body, as if she were now a ghost.

Everything in that world looked a little shimmery, like waves of heat on the embers of a fire. It was the same effect she had seen on ghosts when they had appeared to her in the past, and she realized that this must be the effect of looking through the veil separating the physical world from the astral plane.

"I'm not holding on to him," Cole told her. Suzy directed her attention back to the conversation.

"Maybe not intentionally. But your connection to him is so strong that it's keeping him from waking up."

"He's kind of like me, isn't he?" Cole looked back at Fin.

"In some ways, yes," Suzy agreed. "He comes from a strict religious background. He sometimes feels like he's gone astray from it, and he feels some guilt about that."

"I don't want to hurt anyone." He looked back at Suzy with tears in his eyes. "Anyone else," he amended, likely remembering Laura.

"Then please, Cole, help us. Help Fin! Go through that door and let yourself feel God's love and forgiveness. And it wouldn't hurt to forgive yourself."

Cole actually managed a bit of a smile, the first that Suzy had seen since she had joined him here.

"My, my, who's this?"

Suzy and Cole quickly turned back toward the door – the door into Cole's cell – and saw Sawyer, the guard/orderly, coming through. Cole sighed and put his hand to his face in a regretful gesture.

"I thought I heard voices," Sawyer said, his voice echoing and hollow. His face looked more angular than when Suzy had last seen him in Cole's episode, like skin stretched tightly over a skull. Sawyer licked his lips and hitched his belt up, but was unable to get it over his belly. Suzy thought he looked ridiculous, like Barney Fife with a gut. But having seen a brief sample of his cruelty in Cole's introduction to the place, she realized that, ridiculous or not, he could be a hindrance to her goal.

"Hello, Sawyer," she said, hoping to catch him off guard. She delivered the greeting with a note of coldness in her voice.

"Well, well, you know who I am," he said with a crooked smile, which looked especially harsh under his scowling forehead. "Cole must have been talking about me."

"No, but I've already seen more than I care to."

"Beat it, bonehead," Sawyer said to Cole, apparently ignoring Suzy's brush-off. "I'm gonna show this little lady a good time, then she has to go back to the women's ward."

"She's not from here, Mr. Sawyer," Cole said, still deferring to his demanded title.

"What do you mean, she's not from here?"

"She's alive."

208

Sawyer looked at Cole, the crease between his eyebrows even deeper in his confusion.

"Huh?"

Cole motioned toward the wall of his cell, which dissolved again, to reveal Fin and Suzy in his room in the Spotswood Institute.

"She's not alive if she's here," Sawyer argued.

"Look," Cole said, pointing to Suzy's body, clearly still breathing. "She's alive."

"Well, that's even better! It's been a long time since I've had a *live* woman." Sawyer's sneer returned as he looked Suzy up and down. Despite not being physically connected to her body, Suzy felt her breakfast threatening to come up.

"You don't understand," Cole insisted, "she's obviously very powerful to be able to come here while she's still alive."

Suzy didn't know if Cole actually believed that or not, but she appreciated his attempt to keep Sawyer away from her.

"That pretty little thing?"

Suzy rolled her eyes and sighed disgustedly.

"See that door?" she asked, pointing to the white outline, which was near the opposite wall of the cell now. "Walk up to it, go through it, don't come back."

"How about I walk up to you, go through you a few times and just kind of linger there?"

"She's right, Mr. Sawyer," Cole said. "You need to go now."

"You little shit," Sawyer said, reluctantly turning his attention to Cole, "who are you to tell me what to do?"

"My pop was a preacher," Cole replied. "I remember you crying when your mother died back in '22." Suzy caught a brief look of embarrassment on Sawyer's face. "I know the only way you have any chance of seeing her again is by going through that door."

Sawyer's face twisted into another sneer, the expression that it seemed most comfortable in.

"Maybe I will, maybe I won't." He looked back at Suzy. "But before I do anything, I'm gonna have me a taste of this pretty thing."

Sawyer approached Suzy slowly, and she started backing away from him.

A few years ago, Suzy had faced a threat of rape in a parking garage in Boston. Fortunately, before anything could happen, other people had shown up and the would-be rapist took off. After that, Mark saw to it that she got some self-defense training.

She didn't know what, if anything, any of the suggested moves would do to a ghost. A well-placed kick in the groin might drop a human assailant, but what about a non-corporeal being who had no physical testicles?

She stopped when she came up against the wall of the cell, but as Sawyer got closer to her, she felt herself slip through the wall. With the sudden knowledge that she was closer to where Fin was, the dingy cell next door disappeared and she could see Fin's room.

Her attention was now divided. Sawyer was a nuisance, certainly, but she was more concerned about Fin, as she saw other people in the room now. Her two hours must be up.

She noticed that Peter was there, leaning over Fin, along with a couple of nurses. Drs. Ivanov and Weinberg were at the door speaking quietly between themselves while supervising the medical staff. All of them, from Suzy's point of view, had that rippling glowing ember effect.

Again, Suzy was concerned about the effects their attempts at reviving Fin might have on him while he was still linked to the spirit world. She was upset that Ivanov was going ahead with this, although she realized that it was the deal she had made with him. She had, apparently, taken too long.

In her quick survey of the room, she saw that Peter had noticed that Suzy – physical Suzy – was breathing fast, slumped over in her chair. Since Fin wasn't in any kind of distress, Peter turned his attention to Suzy, holding her wrist to take her pulse.

While she quickly saw what was going on, though, she found that Sawyer had not been distracted, and had not stopped. He grabbed her and pulled her up tight against him.

Suzy tried to push him away, but he held on. With the push, though, she had put just enough distance between their bodies that she was able to swing her knee up to his crotch. Sawyer jerked, but it was likely only an old, instinctive reaction, a leftover memory from life. He didn't let go of her, and his face never registered pain. Instead, he smiled a twisted smile at her.

He held on tightly to one of her arms as he started fumbling with her clothes. Still, she was more concerned about Fin, and Sawyer was just making her angry. Since he had let go with one hand so he could try to undress her, she had a free arm now. She shoved him away as hard as she could, but he just came back as determined as ever.

"Oh for fuck's sake, Sawyer!" she exclaimed, infuriated, "leave me alone!"

Suddenly, she was surrounded by fire, and she thought that Cole was panicking and having another vision of hell and it was bleeding through once again to her consciousness. Then she thought that it was Sawyer responding to her rejection.

It took a second for Suzy to realize that it was actually her. She had erupted in flames, as she had seen Fiona and other ghosts do in the past when they were emotionally charged. From the stunned look on Sawyer's face, and his backing away from her, she assumed that he had not yet discovered that ability. Over his shoulder, she saw Cole, displaying a similar reaction.

Suzy saw an opportunity here.

"You keep being a shit to everybody you see," she said, "and this is what you have to look forward to. An eternity in hell!" She leaned toward him, flaring up as if someone had fanned the flames. Sawyer backed away from her. She noticed the white outline of the door to her right, and she pointed at it.

"Make your last act on earth a good one," she continued, "and maybe you can avoid that. Who knows? Maybe you *can* even see your mother again."

Sawyer looked where she pointed, and the outline began filling in as bright white light poured through the portal. He looked back at Suzy fearfully. He glanced over his shoulder, and for a second, Suzy thought he was going to make a run for it. But he saw Cole there, standing his ground. She doubted that he felt intimidated by Cole, but at least Cole reinforced the command, and the possibility, however slight, that the outcome might, now, turn out a little better for Sawyer.

With a look of resignation on his creased face, Sawyer hesitantly stepped toward the door. The glow enveloped him and, as he crossed the threshold, Sawyer disappeared in a blinding flash as the door closed again, leaving just the white, glowing outline.

As a feeling of relief washed over her, Suzy's flames turned from red to yellow, then flickered out. She looked down at herself, amazed to see herself and the visible representation of her clothing intact and unsinged.

She turned and looked toward Fin, and was shocked to see the staff looking at her. She didn't know at what point the confrontation became visible to them, but without exception, their eyes were wide, their faces ranging from horror to awe to outright excitement.

Suzy wasn't as much of an introvert as Fin was, but still, she never liked to be the center of attention. Self-consciously, she nodded toward them and timidly moved back toward the wall, slipping through it.

That ability, she thought, was equal parts awesome and creepy.

"I've never seen anything like that!" Cole enthused.

"I've seen your hallucinations, Cole," Suzy replied. "I think we both know that's not true."

Cole smiled and nodded. Suzy looked at him for a few moments.

"You're a good man, Cole," she said. His eyes took on the glassy look of being filled with tears.

"You've seen my life," he said, echoing Suzy's earlier thought. "I think we both know that's not true."

"I *have* seen your life," Suzy said. "That's how I know that you're a decent person. You've just had some tough breaks when you were alive." Cole pressed his lips together, as if he was trying to keep from crying. "Were you ever diagnosed here?"

"Dr. Mead said he thought I had something called schizophrenia. It was a mental disease that was discovered right around the time I was brought here. But I wasn't ever given any kind of treatment."

"That's kind of what I thought. A lot of people deal with that these days. But they're not just left to rot and be mistreated in an asylum. I'm so sorry you had to go through that."

The phantom tears in his eyes rolled down his cheeks in response to Suzy's sympathy.

"I meant what I said earlier," she continued, "before we were interrupted. You need to forgive yourself. It wasn't your fault."

"Thank you, Suzy," he said, nodding. He looked toward the white rectangle, which had followed them back into this room. "Well, I guess it's time to face the music."

"I think it'll be a sweeter tune than you're expecting." Suzy smiled at him. Cole chuckled briefly, but his hesitance returned, and he looked back at Suzy.

"If this doesn't work out well," he said, "I'll be blaming you through eternity."

"Fair enough," Suzy chuckled back at him. She put her arms out toward him. Cole looked at her reluctantly for a moment, then he went to her, experiencing an embrace for the first time in over a century.

"You know," Cole said as he continued holding Suzy, "maybe you could come with me."

"Don't push your luck, Cole," Suzy replied as she pushed him away. But she tempered her rejection with another smile.

Cole nodded and smiled nervously as he looked at the glowing white rectangle. He took a deep breath and took a step toward it. Instantly, it opened up and light poured through, flooding the dingy cell with brilliance.

Looking up at Suzy, his forehead was creased as his eyebrows were raised as high as they would go. He looked back at the door and took another step. One more step and the light wrapped around him. Then, he was gone, and the cell was dim again as the door closed up.

§

Suzy sighed as she looked at the white rectangle hanging in the dingy cell.

*It's over. It's finally over.*

As the moments passed, the rectangle still held her scrutiny. But there were some other things that had caught her attention in the last few minutes, as well.

When she had been struggling with Sawyer, her brief memory of almost being raped in the Boston parking garage, and the self-defense lessons afterwards, brought Mark to mind. He had been so horrified when she told him about it, and so relieved that she was alright. But he had also been so concerned about her future safety that he personally booked the lessons for her himself.

Then there was the argument that Cole had made, that Sawyer might be able to see his dead mother again. Suzy was fairly certain that this possibility had played a part in convincing Sawyer to go.

214

Finally, there was something that Cole said to Suzy, just before he went through the portal. He had asked her to come with him.

That was never a temptation. Cole had never meant anything to her in that way. But what if Mark and Emma were over there on the other side of the door? Could she see them again?

She stepped tentatively toward the rectangle, and it opened anew. Standing directly in front of it, she was a little surprised. As intense as the light was, she had almost expected it to be warm. But there was no sensation, other than the brightness of it.

She stood there peering through the portal, trying to see beyond the magnitude of the glare flooding the little cell. If only she could perceive movements, shapes. She wondered if she could recognize her loved ones just by faint silhouettes against the white.

As she stood there, she felt her anxiety building as tears filled her eyes. An immeasurable yearning was growing in her chest, an unbearable need to hold her loved ones. She felt the equivalent of her heart pounding, her breathing intensifying, and she wondered if anyone in the next room had noticed the physical signs of her mounting tension in her slumped body.

Rooted in place, she hesitated, instinctively squinting into the snowy whiteness. As that phrase, 'snowy whiteness,' drifted through her mind, something about that description tickled her brain. She realized that Fin probably couldn't look into it without developing a migraine. Then, a smile pushed through her tears as she pictured him picking up his phone so he could make a note of the phrase to use in his writing.

And she remembered that he was there, just on the other side of the wall, on the flip side of her consciousness. She wondered if Cole's exit from this plane of existence had released Fin from his ghost-induced coma.

She felt torn between wanting to go through the door and wanting to stay. In a sense, she was two people right now, her consciousness here, and her body in the next room. She wished she could choose both.

She knew what she had here, but she also knew what she had lost three years ago. If only Rachel were here to advise her.

And the thought of Rachel, in addition to Fin, made the tears flow all over again.

## 48

No, I'm not thirsty," Fin insisted impatiently to Peter. He turned to the nurse next to him. "I'm not hungry. No, I don't have any pain. I'm fine!"

The nurse persisted, though.

"We're just concerned," she said defensively. "You've been unconscious for a while, and your heart rate and blood pressure are elevated."

"Ya think? After what I just saw, I think that's pretty normal. I'm more concerned about her, though," Fin motioned toward Suzy, still slumped in her chair.

"He's right," Dr. Weinberg said as she stepped forward to his bed. "Why don't we leave him alone and let him catch his breath."

Peter and the nurse nodded and began gathering up the things they had brought with them. Dr. Ivanov stayed by the door, but Dr. Weinberg addressed Fin now.

"What about her?" she asked quietly, indicating Suzy. "Does she need help? Should we do anything?"

"I have no idea," Fin said, feeling a little lost. "She's never done that before. She always just watched and communicated. She's never actually participated on their level before."

"I would have been absolutely terrified!" the nurse said to Fin, depositing her things on the tray she had brought in. Her face still showed some of the horror she felt when the ghosts showed up in the room.

"That was SO incredible!" Peter said, much more enthusiastically.

Fin was only partly aware of what they were saying. He could see Suzy finally starting to stir.

"Ms. Quinn," Dr. Weinberg said as she knelt down beside the chair, "are you alright? Do you need anything?"

Suzy pushed herself up in the chair and looked around her, seeing the same faces she had seen a few minutes ago.

"No, thank you," she replied quietly, a little nervously. "I'm fine."

"Alright. Well," Dr. Weinberg stood back up, gently squeezing Suzy's shoulder, "Fin seems to be fine, too. We were just about to leave him alone to rest."

Responding to her signal, Peter and the nurse picked up their things to go. As they walked past Suzy, they both looked at her deferentially. Peter couldn't seem to contain himself, though.

"Girl, you were amazing!"

"Thank you," Suzy reddened. She looked at Fin. "I didn't realize it was going to be a public performance," she said quietly.

She watched as they filed out, and she saw Dr. Ivanov standing there by the door. The arrogance she had last seen on his face was gone.

"Ees good to have you back," he said quietly, almost humbly.

"Thank you." Suzy managed a tired smile as Dr. Ivanov closed the door, leaving her and Fin alone.

She wearily pushed herself up from her chair and sat down on the edge of Fin's bed. Fin scooted over against the rail and pulled her down beside him, holding her with his free right arm.

"Honey," Suzy said, "are you really okay?"

"Absolutely!" he replied, his voice saturated with relief. "I'm fine. Especially now that you're back." He kissed her and studied her face. "What about you? That was some pretty intense shit you did!"

"Oh, they told you about that, huh?"

"Told me about it? I saw it."

"What?" Suzy looked at him, confused. "You were still unconscious when I came through the wall."

"I saw it all, from when you first appeared in front of Cole, to the moment he stepped through the door. I saw it through his eyes."

"Oh my god!" Suzy's eyes widened. "You saw through his eyes as he went into the light? What did it look like?"

"It was bright." Suzy smiled, remembering her thoughts about Fin and the 'snowy whiteness' phrase. "But I didn't see anything of the other side. As soon as Cole stepped into the light, I came to. It was as if somebody pulled the plug and my connection to him was broken."

He held her tightly against him and chuckled.

"What?" Suzy asked, craning her head back to look at him.

"You're such a badass. My vixen from hell!"

§

"As you probably know, there is no known cure for migraines," Dr. Weinberg said as she sat behind her desk in her office reviewing Fin's case. Fin sat in front of her desk, his crutch lying on the floor beside him. Suzy sat on his left, listening to the prognosis with him. "There are only tricks and treatments, to address the symptoms."

"Like Mizaide," Fin said ruefully.

"Exactly. And you were clever enough to discover that that's not a viable option for you.

"That said, there are a couple of things that can be done to prevent them, or at least lessen the severity of them. And I'll warn you ahead of time, they might seem like a bit of an anticlimax, but many patients have had success with them."

She stood up, picking up a little device from her desk.

"You're right-handed, aren't you?" she asked as she came around her desk toward Fin. He nodded. "Okay, this goes on your non-dominant hand, so your cast will complicate things for a while. But I'll demonstrate it on your right hand.

"This is really nothing more than a little plastic clip." She inserted a finger between the two ends to separate them and slid them over the web of skin and muscle between Fin's thumb and forefinger. "There's an amazing little pressure point in this location that will lessen the pain of a headache, or even make it go away. But again, you'll have to use it in this spot on your left hand when you get your cast off."

"Okay," Fin nodded.

"Secondly, if a headache does get started," she continued as she went back around to her chair, "an over-the-counter pain reliever, taken with coffee or tea, may provide relief."

"Taken with coffee or tea?" Suzy asked.

"Yes, caffeine constricts the blood vessels, which in itself can provide relief for headaches. Migraines are generally more intense than your run-of-the-mill headache, so doubling up with the pain reliever can help to kick it. Hemp oil is a really good one, too, if you're into natural therapies.

"Finally," she picked up a few printed sheets of paper, and handed them to Fin, "we've put together a few exercises that may help as well. Also, yoga and meditation are highly recommended."

"Huh," Fin said, glancing over the prints.

"Like I said," Dr. Weinberg acknowledged, "it may seem a little anti-climactic, but since you can't take Mizaide, we think this will give you some relief. Along with staying inside, if you can, when it's particularly bright, since you know that's your main trigger.

"And I can personally guarantee that not one of these therapies will cause hallucinations. So hopefully, you can have a happy holiday season. What's left of it, anyway."

"What is today?" Fin asked.

"It's the 24th," Suzy replied.

"Yes," Dr. Weinberg said, "that's why I'm here and Dr. Ivanov is at home with his family."

"Thank you, doctor," Fin nodded.

# 49

Ursula lay curled up in Suzy's lap on the love seat in Fin's library. Suzy had been petting her for nearly an hour while she and Fin talked about their adventures over the last few days. Fin sat next to her, his right leg extended in front of him and resting on an ottoman.

"I can't believe I'm actually jealous of my dog," he said.

Suzy smiled.

"You can curl up in my lap later," she promised.

"'kay," Fin smiled.

Fin's mind drifted back to their on-again-off-again conversation about Cole.

"Do you think there are other ghosts in the Spotswood Institute?"

"I wouldn't be a bit surprised. The asylum was in operation for over forty years. Even outside the flu epidemic, I would think that quite a few people died there."

"You think it's swarming with ghosts?"

"No. Most of them likely went through the door into the light right away. But it wouldn't surprise me if a few stuck around like Cole and Sawyer."

They passed a few more moments of quiet closeness.

"Are you ever going to turn on the lights on your tree?" Suzy asked, looking at his sad, dark little tree in the corner.

"I had them on earlier, and my house burned down."

"I guess I don't have any room to talk. Rachel called my tree anemic. Christmas was always a big deal with Mark and Emma. Living by myself, now, I almost don't see the point."

"Kind of the same with me, except for different reasons. Christmas was *never* a big deal with my family. The commercialized celebration of the birth of Christ on a day that wasn't his birthday, but rather a Roman celebration, with pagan trappings that go back way before Christianity? Yeah, that didn't go over real well."

His mind was still in their earlier conversation, though. After a few moments, as a thought occurred to him, his expression became a little more pensive.

"You know," he said, "we looked up the Springers, and their part in the beginnings of Highlands Ranch, and about the murder. But there's one thing I'm still wondering. Do you think Cole's affair with Isabel was real?"

Suzy shook her head as she pondered the question.

"I don't know. Considering his hallucinated affair with Laura, it's hard to say. I'm not sure if Cole could even say for certain."

Fin nodded.

"I suppose it might be possible, given her historically established unfaithfulness and promiscuity," he said. "But I'm not sure how likely an affluent woman back then would be to take up with one of her servants."

They were quiet for a few moments until Suzy embarked on a new subject.

"So, what are you going to do for a car?" she asked.

"Well, how long are you going to be here?"

"Ah, my lifelong dreams of running a taxi service have finally come true."

"Fact is," Fin smiled, "I'm kind of a hermit. I don't really have many places to go. I suppose after you leave, I can call Uber if I need to, until I get my cast off and can get another car."

He sighed and frowned.

"By the way, how long *are* you going to be here?"

"I dunno," she shrugged noncommittally and leaned against Fin. He didn't mind.

"Actually, driving is kind of the least of my worries at the moment." He looked at the papers that Dr. Weinberg had given him. "In my previous life, yoga was always forbidden. It was considered a possible link to Hindu gods, so it was considered pagan."

"Are you okay with it now?" Suzy asked.

"It's fine. I've gone astray, remember? But I don't know anything about yoga or meditation."

"I can help you with that."

"That's a nice offer, but you live two thousand miles away, in Massa-freakin-chusetts. Are you going to stick around here until my casts come off? Because I kind of doubt I'll be getting myself in the lotus position as long as I have this thing on." He knocked on his leg cast, and Ursula lifted her head and looked around.

"Well, no," Suzy replied, "I doubt I'll be here that long."

"And wouldn't you know it," Fin continued, "bright light is my main trigger for migraines, and I live in a place with over three hundred sunny days a year, and a thinner atmosphere to filter it."

"Like I said, I think I can help with that."

Fin looked at her.

"What are you talking about?"

Suzy left a long pause as she pondered the fur on Ursula's back. Finally, she looked at Fin.

"A year and a half ago, after we got back from Scotland," she said, "you were talking about possibly selling your house and moving to Marblehead."

"Right," Fin nodded, "I remember. And you convinced me I was being a doltish numpty. Or something like that."

"Yeah, well, that was then. We hadn't known each other very long. Since then, we've spent some more time together, had a couple of adventures, for better or worse, and I think I might be ready to take the next step."

"You want to tie the knot, huh?" Fin asked with a smile, knowing he was pushing her buttons.

"Maybe in time," Suzy said with a sigh, staying focused. "For now, though, if it still appeals to you, maybe you could consider moving someplace that has a little less sun and a thicker sea-level atmosphere."

"You want me to move out there?" Fin asked, finally becoming serious.

"I want you to do what feels right to you. But if moving to Marblehead feels right, you have a place to live."

"You want to put me in your formerly haunted, murder-scene carriage house, don't you?"

"No, I'm thinking about putting that up as an Airbnb. I was thinking you could stay in the main house."

Fin looked at her for a few moments.

"Honey, are you asking me to move in with you?"

Focusing on petting Ursula, Suzy took a long, deep breath, and blew it out.

"Yeah, I guess I am."

"What about all the memories of Mark in the house?"

She glanced briefly at Fin.

"Well, like I told you a few days ago on the phone, I'm having the house renovated. Part of it is about making it more authentic to its original style, since seeing the episodes of Fiona living there. But part of it was to strip away some of those reminders."

"Are you sure you're okay with that," Fin asked, surprised, "stripping out those memories?"

"Well, as my very wise friend, Rachel, pointed out, the decorations are not the same as memories. They're like a bookmark, physical reminders of certain events." She looked up at Fin, peering at him for a few moments. "Those memories are a part of me. They'll always be with me. I hope you're okay with that."

Fin smiled at her and leaned his head against hers.

"I think I told you once that I thought it would be easier for me if your husband had been an asshole, and that you had divorced him, instead of him dying while you still loved him. At the same time, I would never want to wish that unhappiness on you."

"Not that losing him was a happy memory."

"No, of course not. But you do have a lot of happy memories up until then. He and Emma are a part of your life, your history. Your loved ones and your experiences, good and bad, and how you've dealt with them, are what made you the woman I love now."

"Good answer," Suzy leaned into him and kissed him.

Fin spent a few pleasant moments pondering living with Suzy in Massachusetts, and he couldn't help smiling. And living in an old historic landmark could be fun, too.

"You don't have any more ghosts out there, do you?" he asked. "I think I've had enough of this SpiritSense shit for a while."

"*I* don't have any," Suzy replied with a teasing, nonchalant tone, "but who knows where else the rest of our lives might take us?"

# Notes and Acknowledgments

I learned a great deal of historical information from the book *Murder at the Brown Palace* by Dick Kreck. Many of the details that found their way into my story came from this book and from phone calls to the author. (Only a couple – I'm not a pest!)

For personal, one-on-one information and encouragement, I'd like to thank Susie Appleby and Todd Noreen at the Highlands Ranch Mansion. Your enthusiasm and support were invaluable. (Susie, you need to get back to writing *your* book!)

We introverted creative types can be a sensitive lot. We need encouragement and confirmation that what we're doing really is as good as we think it is. Sometimes we need oh-so-gentle critiques and suggestions to make what we're doing better. My wife, Linda does this so well, helping me keep my work on track, while keeping my self-esteem intact. Being a creative type herself, I can only hope that whatever support *I* provide is as helpful to her.

Finally, readers are essential to a writer. I sometimes get positive personal feedback, and I'm not going to downplay that at all. It's always very nice. But it doesn't spread the word. **If you like what you've read, please consider leaving a brief review at Amazon and/or Goodreads.**

Made in the USA
Coppell, TX
06 June 2020